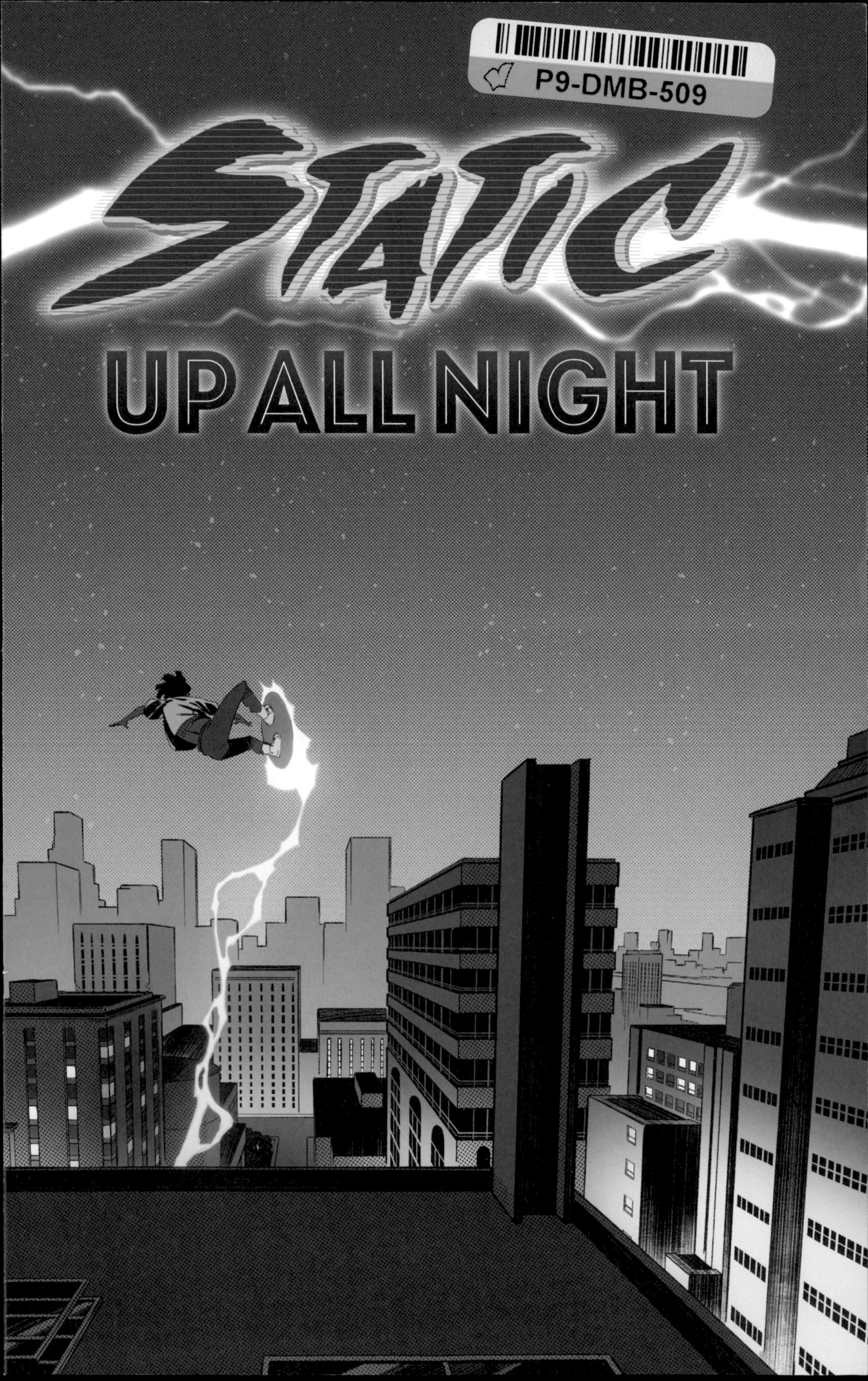
STATIC
UP ALL NIGHT

STATIC

UP ALL NIGHT

Written by
Lamar Giles

Art by
Paris Alleyne
with
N. Steven Harris

Colored by **Bex Glendining**

Letters by **AndWorld Design**

STATIC created by **DWAYNE McDUFFIE, DEREK T. DINGLE, DENYS COWAN,** and **MICHAEL DAVIS**

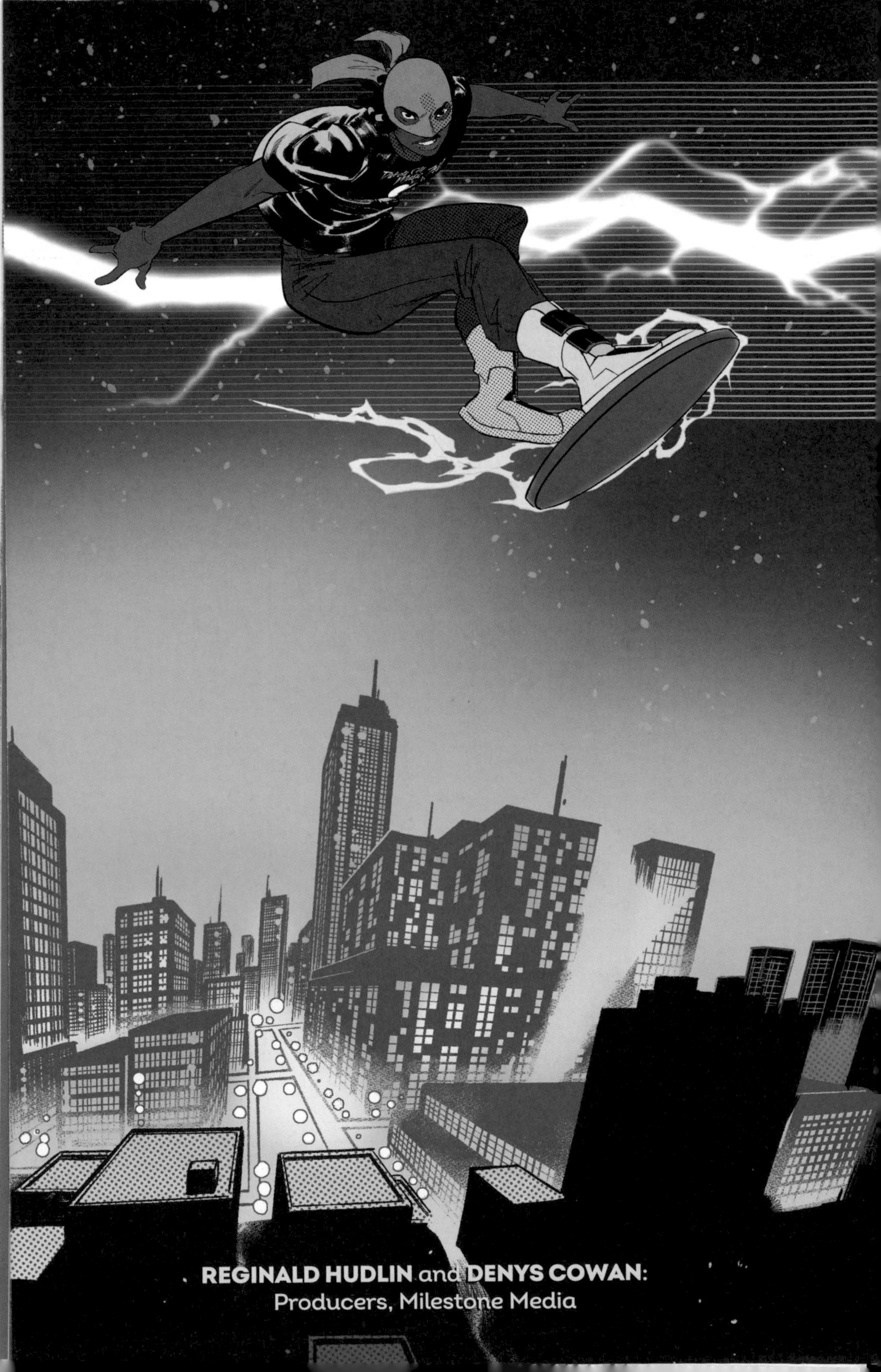
REGINALD HUDLIN and **DENYS COWAN:**
Producers, Milestone Media

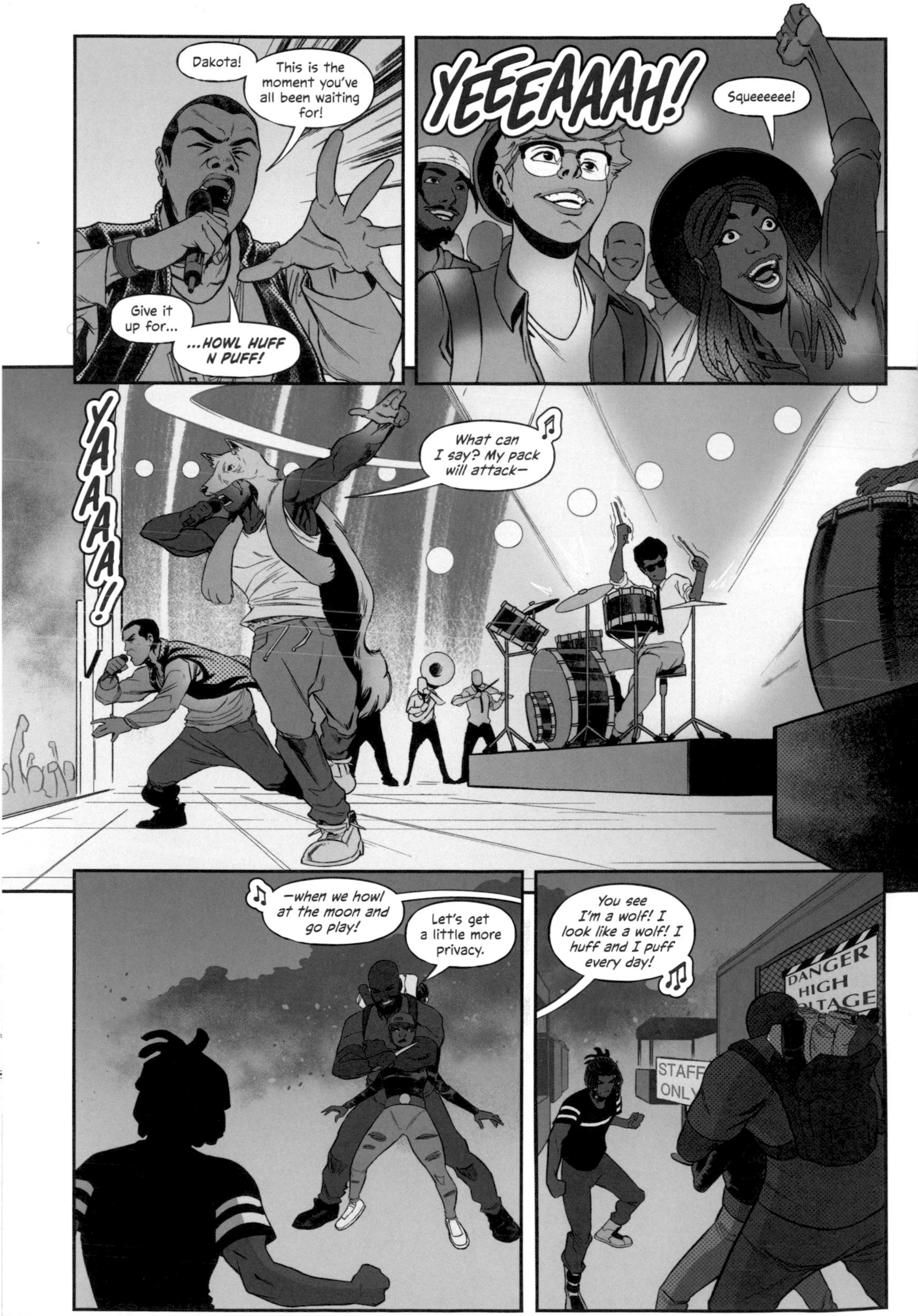

Dakota!
This is the moment you've all been waiting for!
Give it up for...
...HOWL HUFF N PUFF!
YEEEAAAAH!
Squeeeeee!
YAAAAA!!
What can I say? My pack will attack—
—when we howl at the moon and go play!
Let's get a little more privacy.
You see I'm a wolf! I look like a wolf! I huff and I puff every day!
DANGER HIGH VOLTAGE
STAFF ONLY

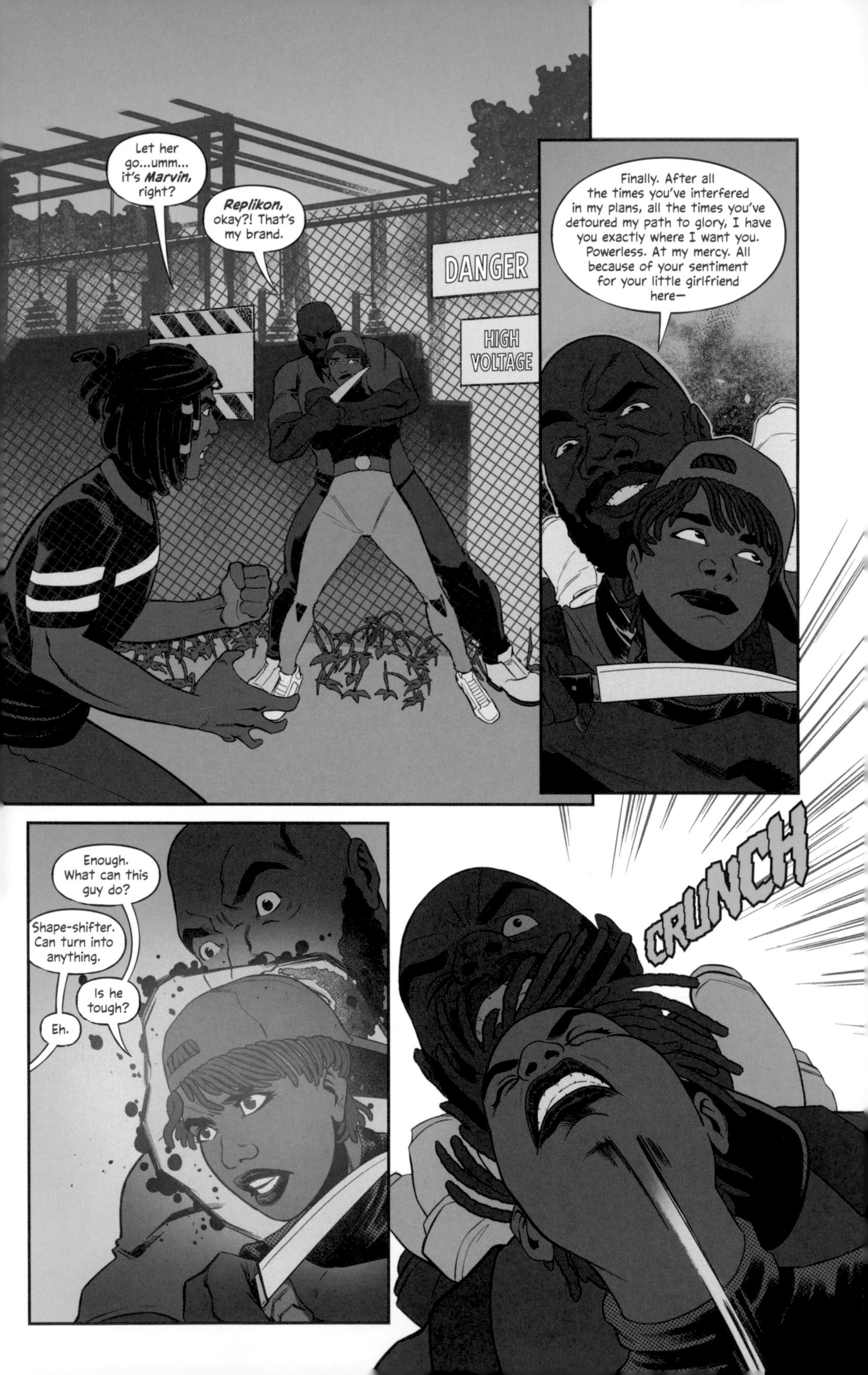
Let her go...umm... it's **Marvin,** right?
Replikon, okay?! That's my brand.
DANGER
HIGH VOLTAGE
Finally. After all the times you've interfered in my plans, all the times you've detoured my path to glory, I have you exactly where I want you. Powerless. At my mercy. All because of your sentiment for your little girlfriend here—
Enough. What can this guy do?
Shape-shifter. Can turn into anything.
Is he tough?
Eh.
CRUNCH

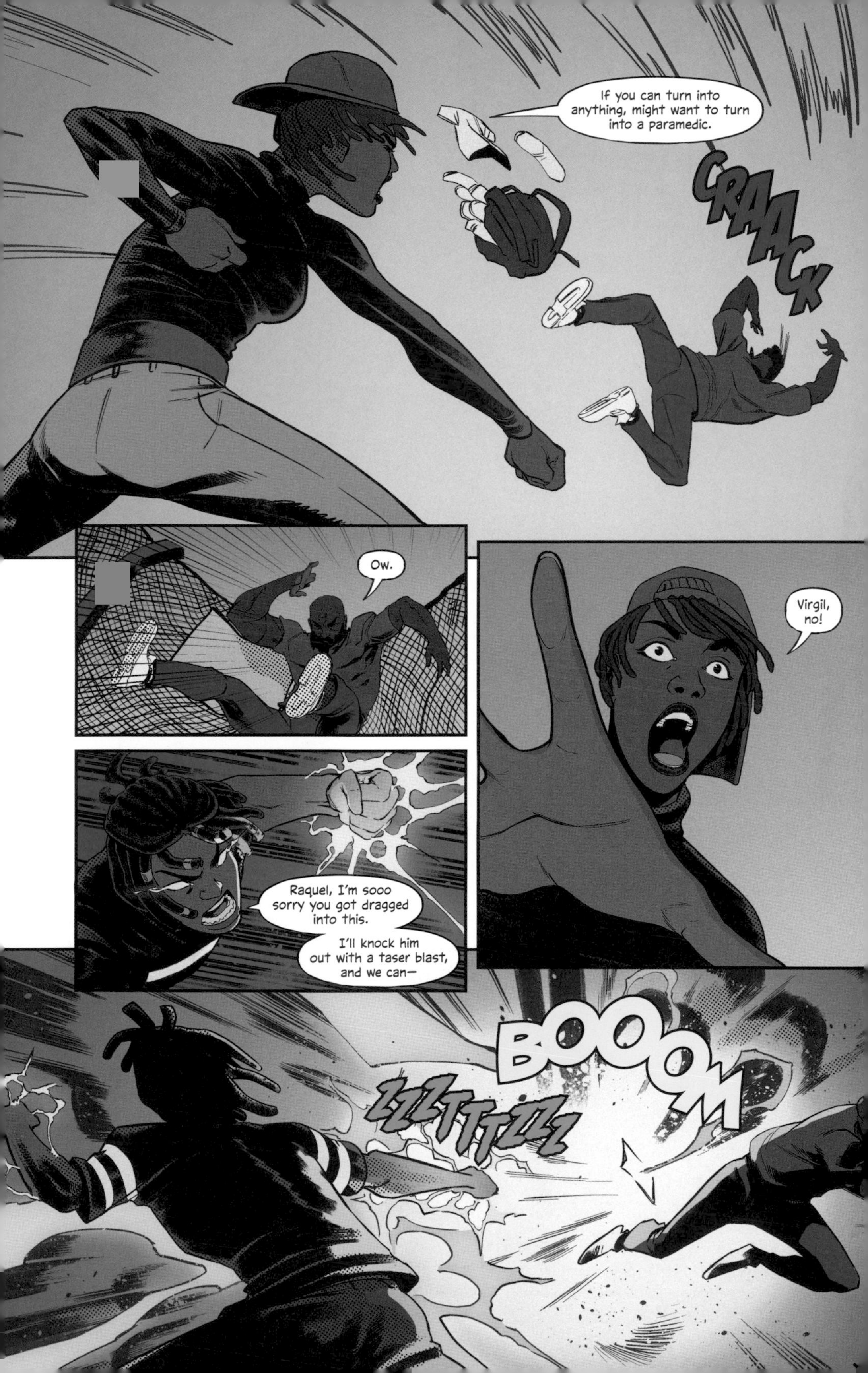
If you can turn into anything, might want to turn into a paramedic.
CRAAACK
Ow.
Virgil, no!
Raquel, I'm sooo sorry you got dragged into this.
I'll knock him out with a taser blast, and we can—
BOOOOM
ZZZTTTZZZ

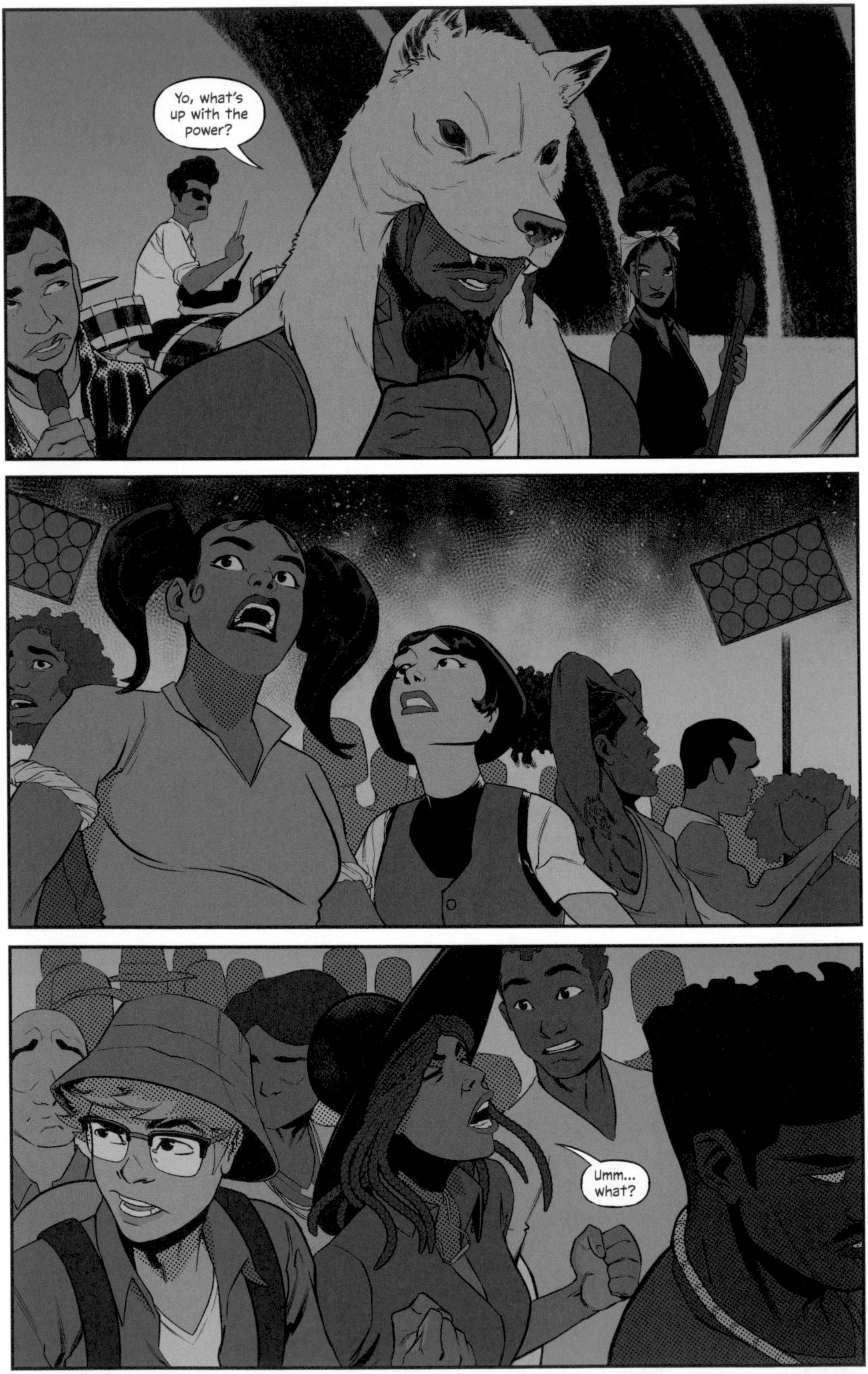
Yo, what's up with the power?
Umm... what?

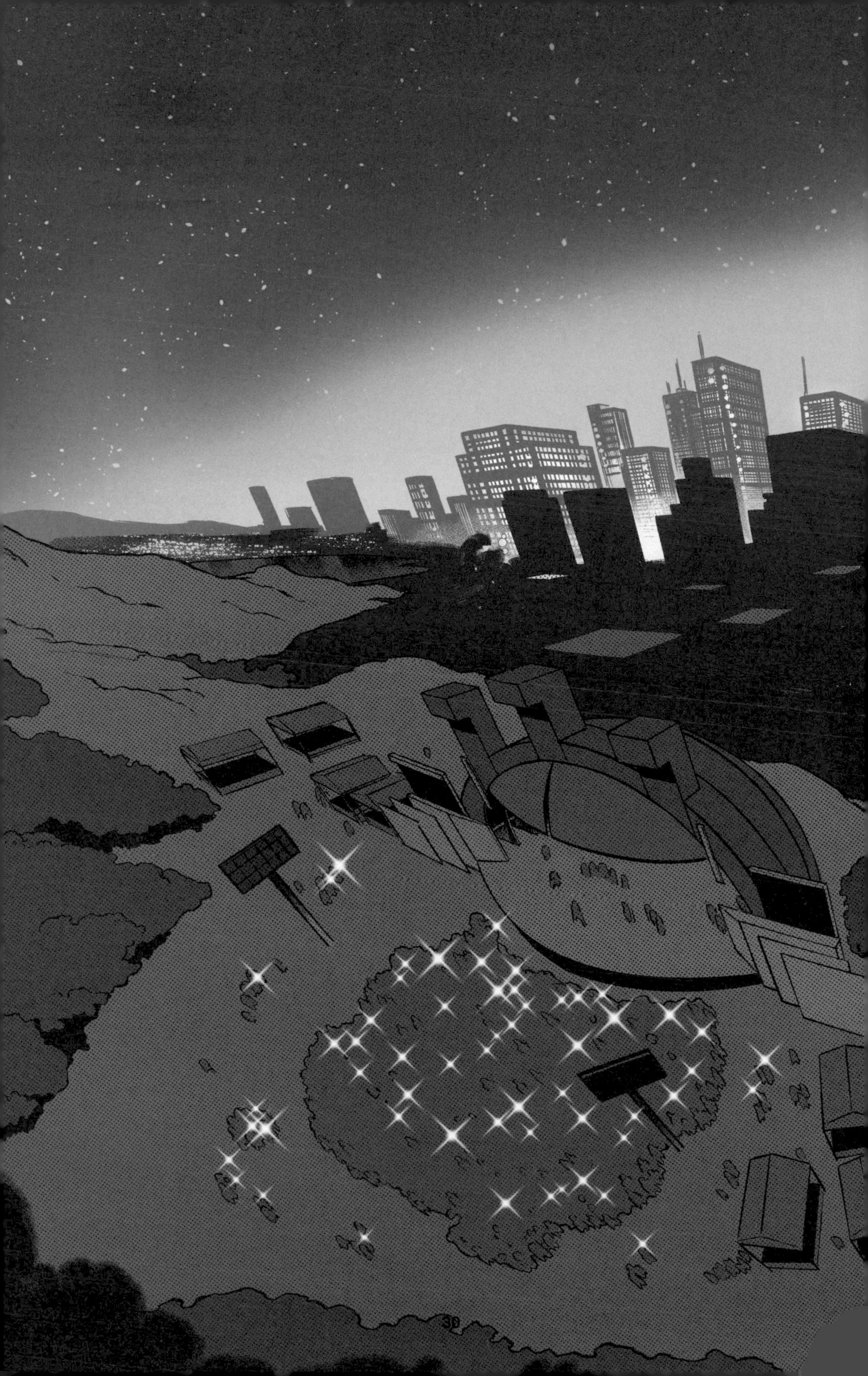

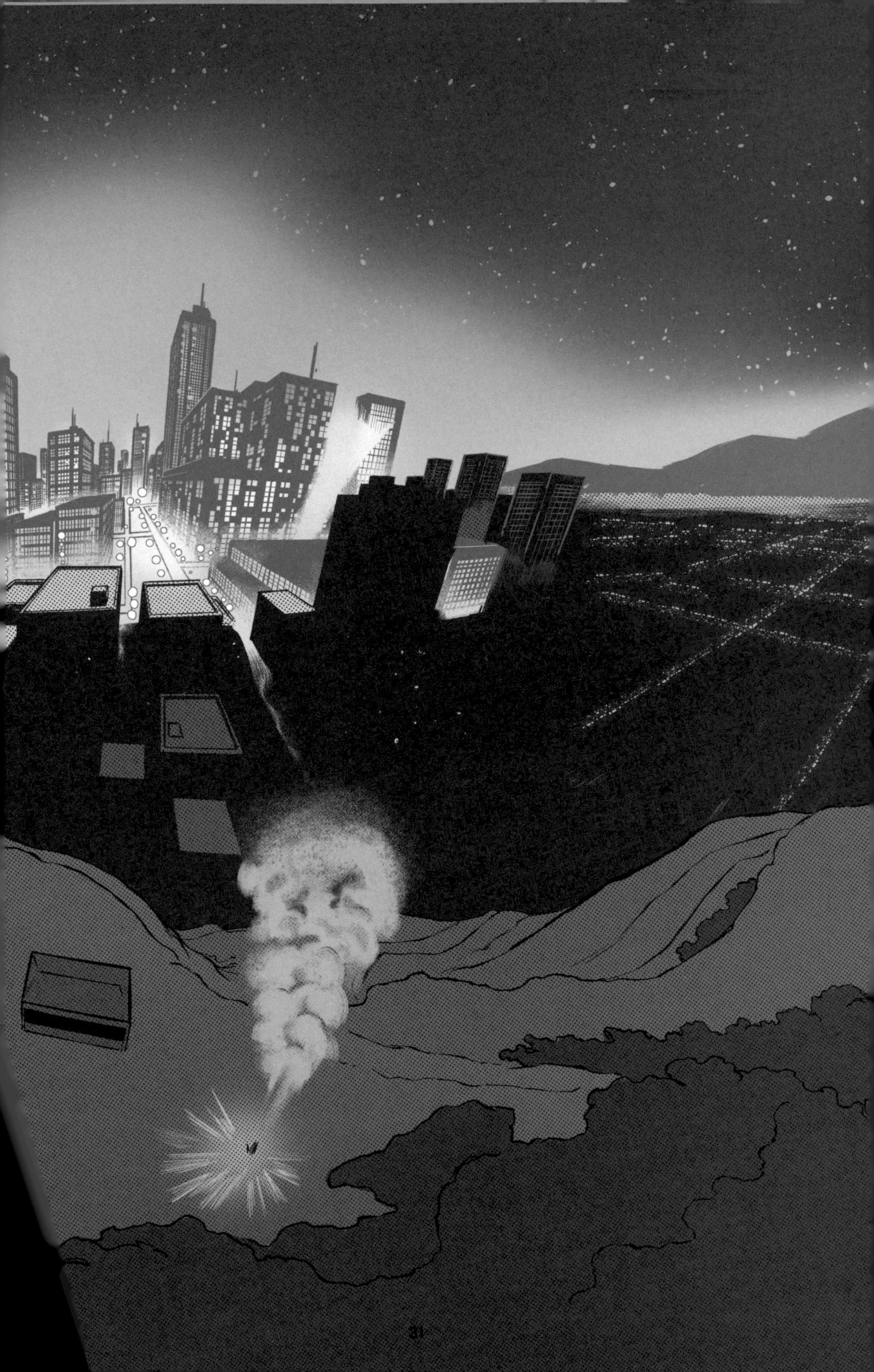

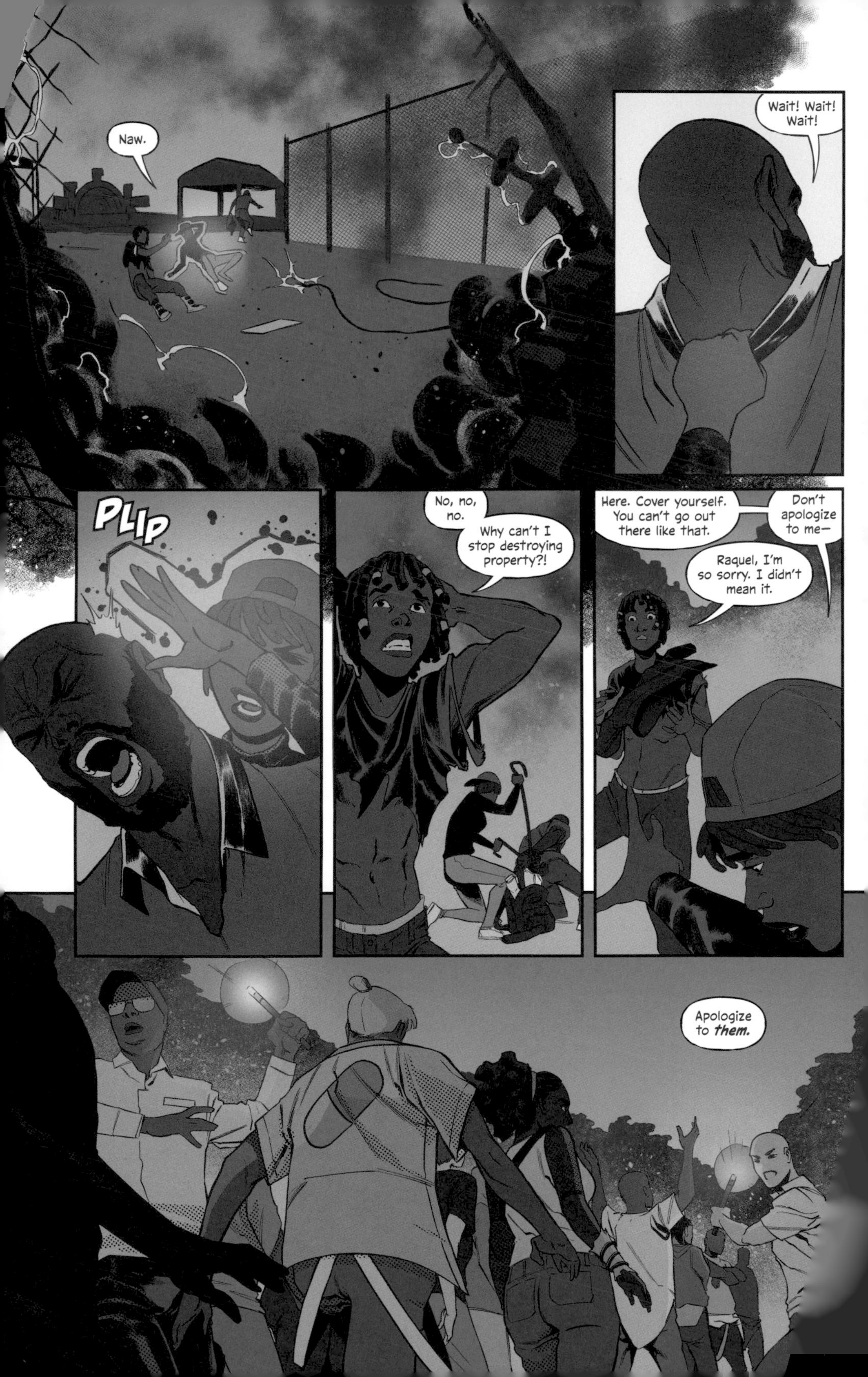
Naw.
Wait! Wait! Wait!
PLIP
No, no, no.
Why can't I stop destroying property?!
Here. Cover yourself. You can't go out there like that.
Raquel, I'm so sorry. I didn't mean it.
Don't apologize to me—
Apologize to *them.*

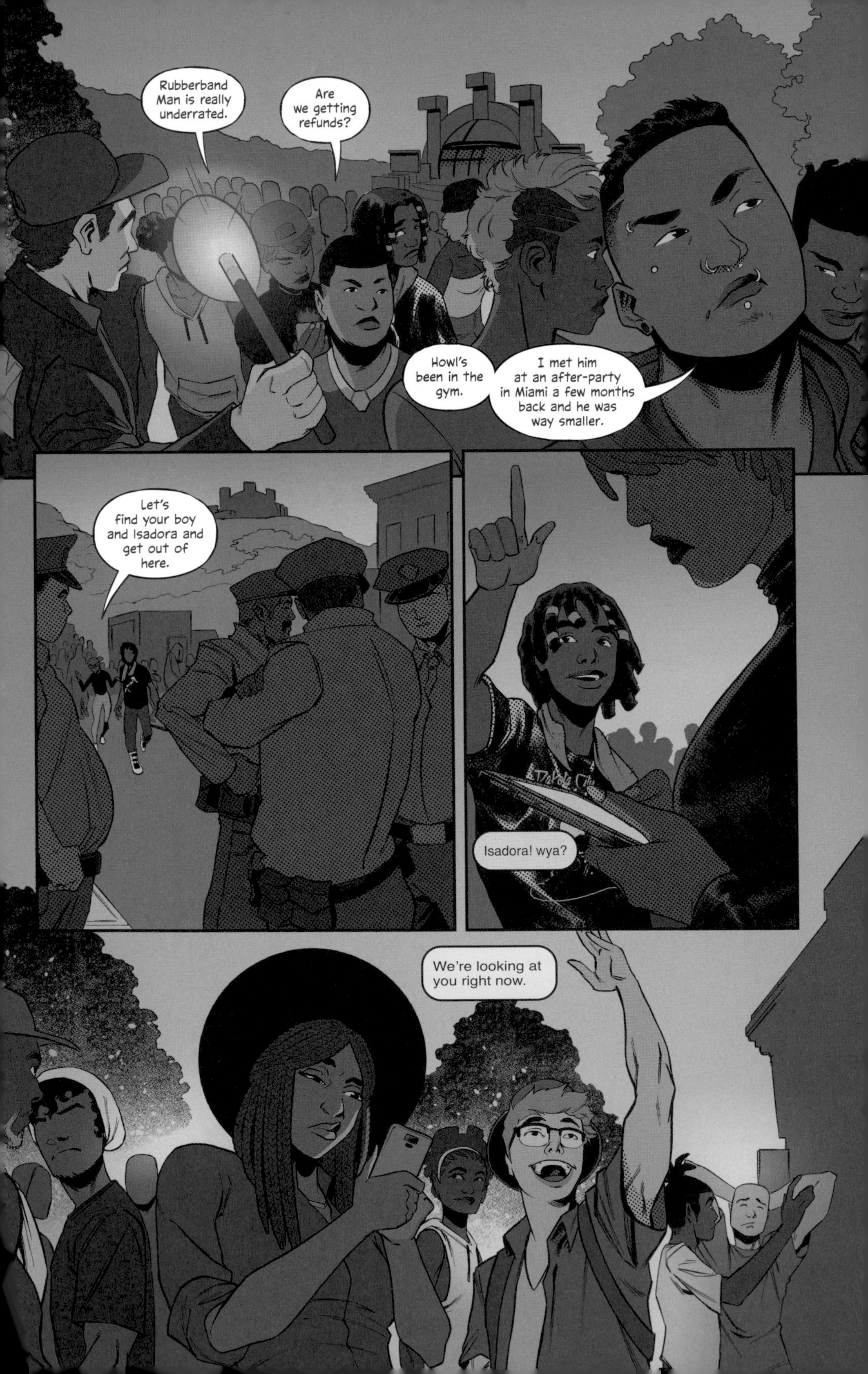
Rubberband Man is really underrated.
Are we getting refunds?
Howl's been in the gym.
I met him at an after-party in Miami a few months back and he was way smaller.
Let's find your boy and Isadora and get out of here.
Isadora! wya?
We're looking at you right now.

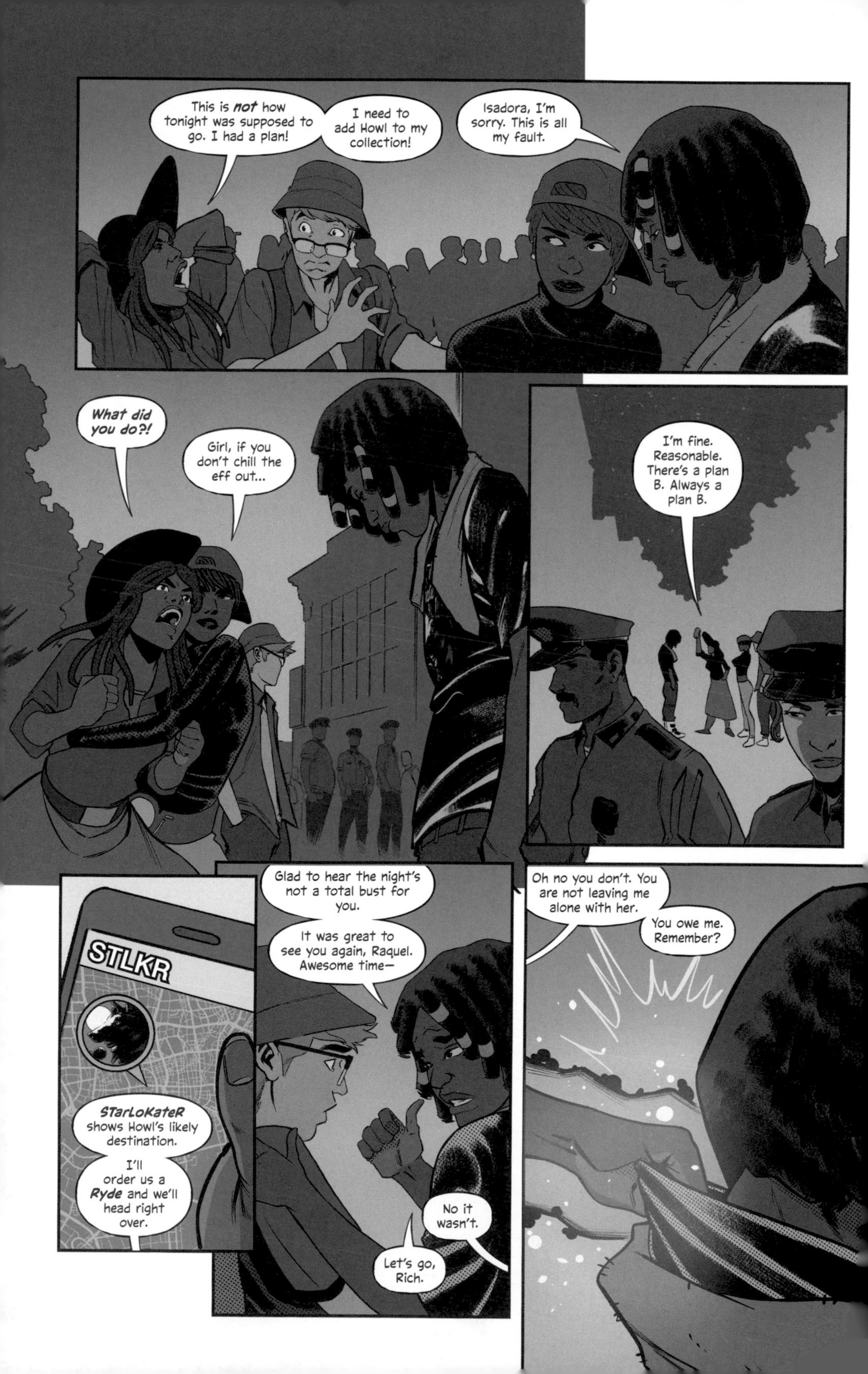
This is *not* how tonight was supposed to go. I had a plan!
I need to add Howl to my collection!
Isadora, I'm sorry. This is all my fault.
What did you do?!
Girl, if you don't chill the eff out...
I'm fine. Reasonable. There's a plan B. Always a plan B.
STLKR
STarLoKateR shows Howl's likely destination.
I'll order us a *Ryde* and we'll head right over.
Glad to hear the night's not a total bust for you.
It was great to see you again, Raquel. Awesome time—
No it wasn't.
Let's go, Rich.
Oh no you don't. You are not leaving me alone with her.
You owe me. Remember?

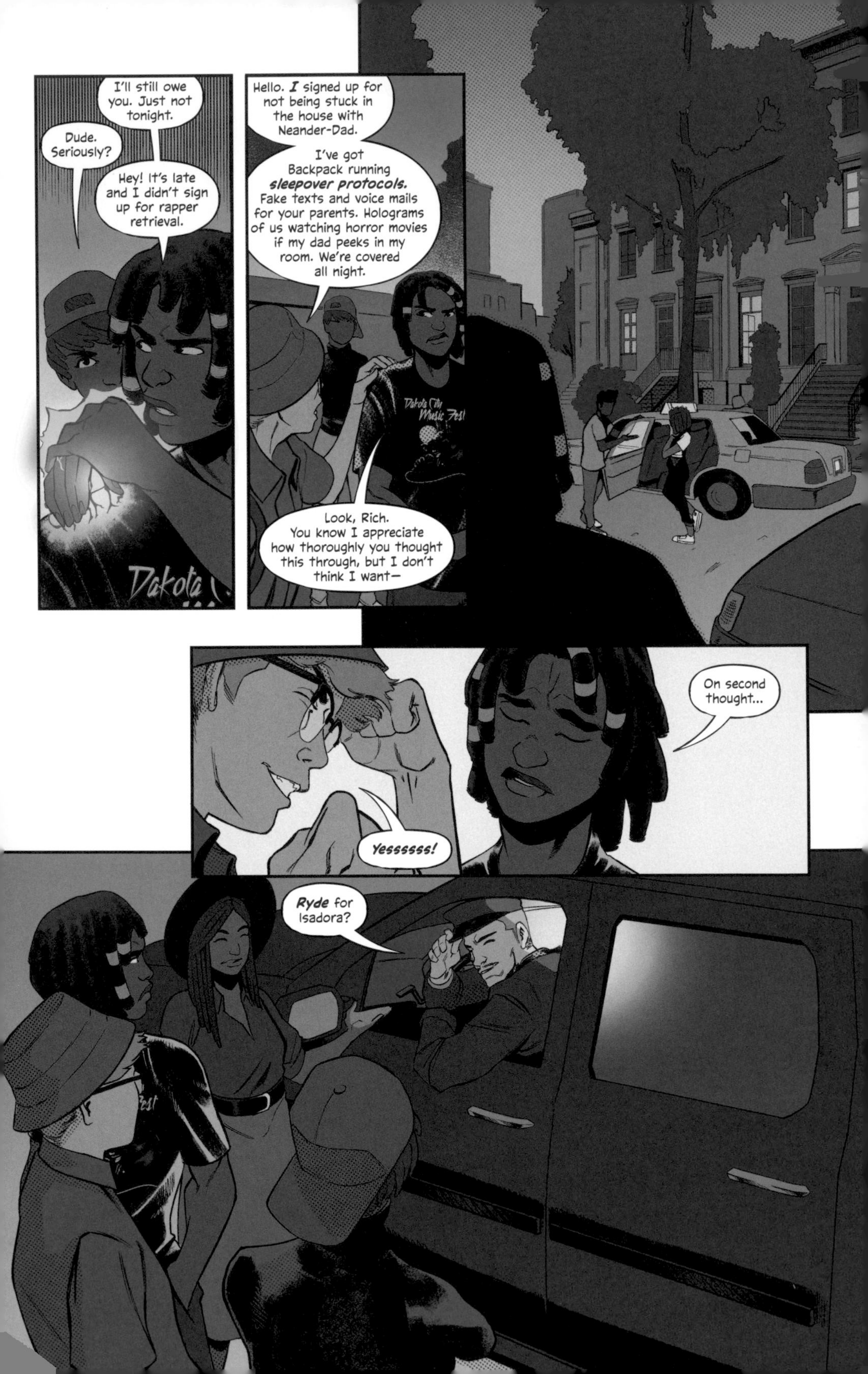
I'll still owe you. Just not tonight.
Dude. Seriously?
Hey! It's late and I didn't sign up for rapper retrieval.
Dakota
Hello. *I* signed up for not being stuck in the house with Neander-Dad.
I've got Backpack running ***sleepover protocols.*** Fake texts and voice mails for your parents. Holograms of us watching horror movies if my dad peeks in my room. We're covered all night.
Dakota City Music Fest
Look, Rich. You know I appreciate how thoroughly you thought this through, but I don't think I want—
On second thought...
Yessssss!
Ryde for Isadora?

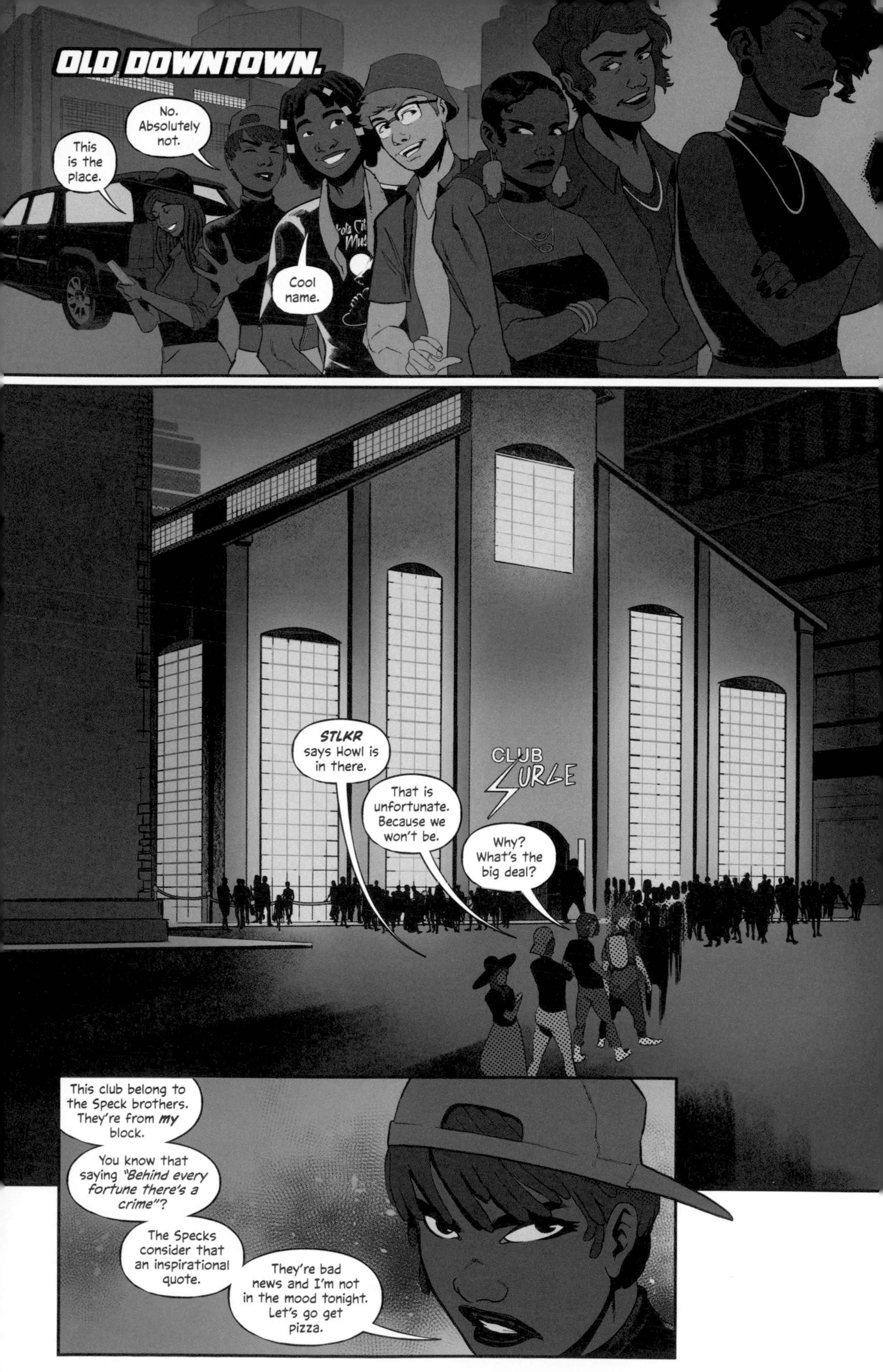
OLD DOWNTOWN.
This is the place.
No. Absolutely not.
Cool name.
STLKR says Howl is in there.
CLUB SURGE
That is unfortunate. Because we won't be.
Why? What's the big deal?
This club belong to the Speck brothers. They're from my block.
You know that saying "Behind every fortune there's a crime"?
The Specks consider that an inspirational quote.
They're bad news and I'm not in the mood tonight. Let's go get pizza.

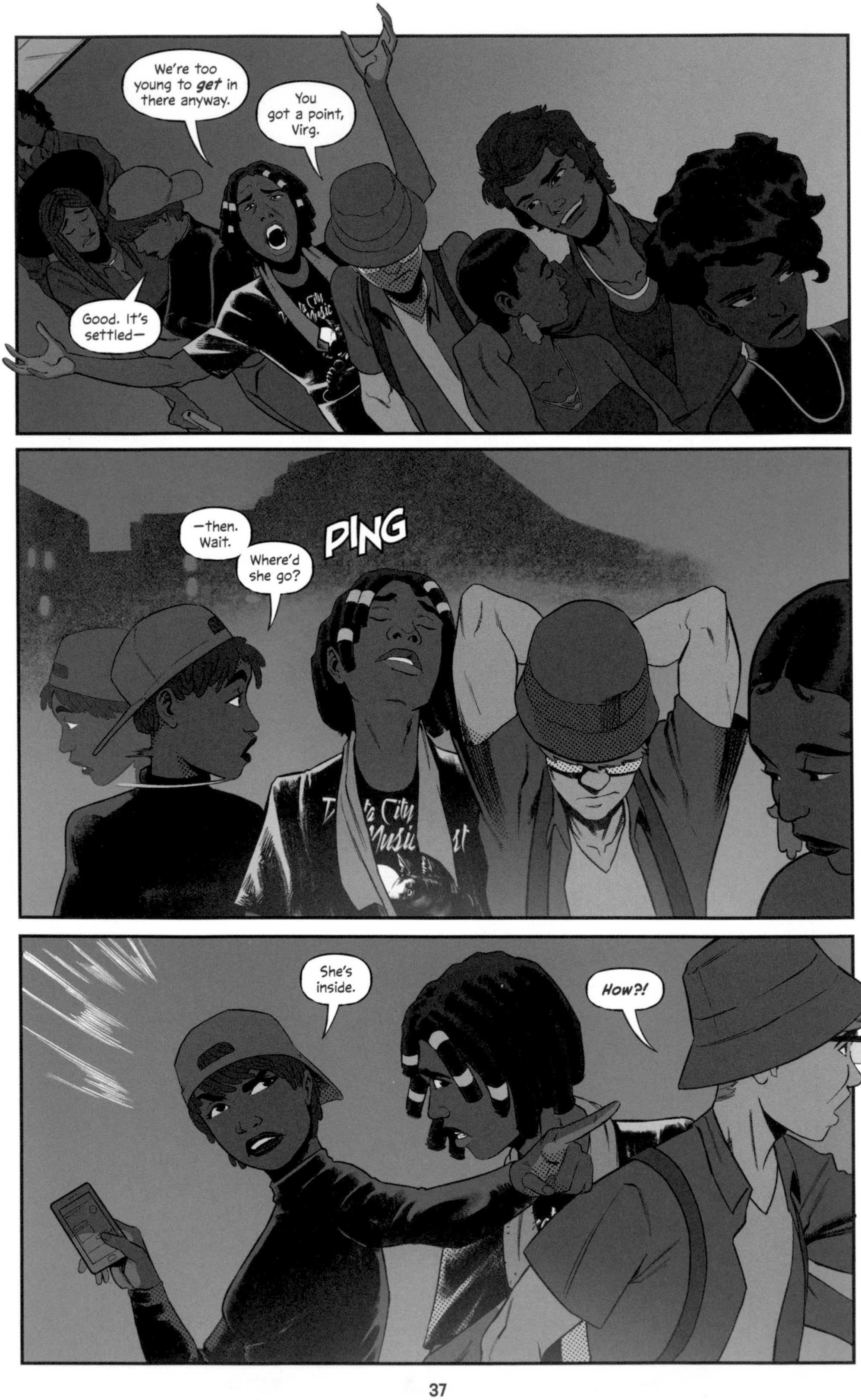
We're too young to get in there anyway.
You got a point, Virg.
Good. It's settled—
—then. Wait.
Where'd she go?
PING
She's inside.
How?!

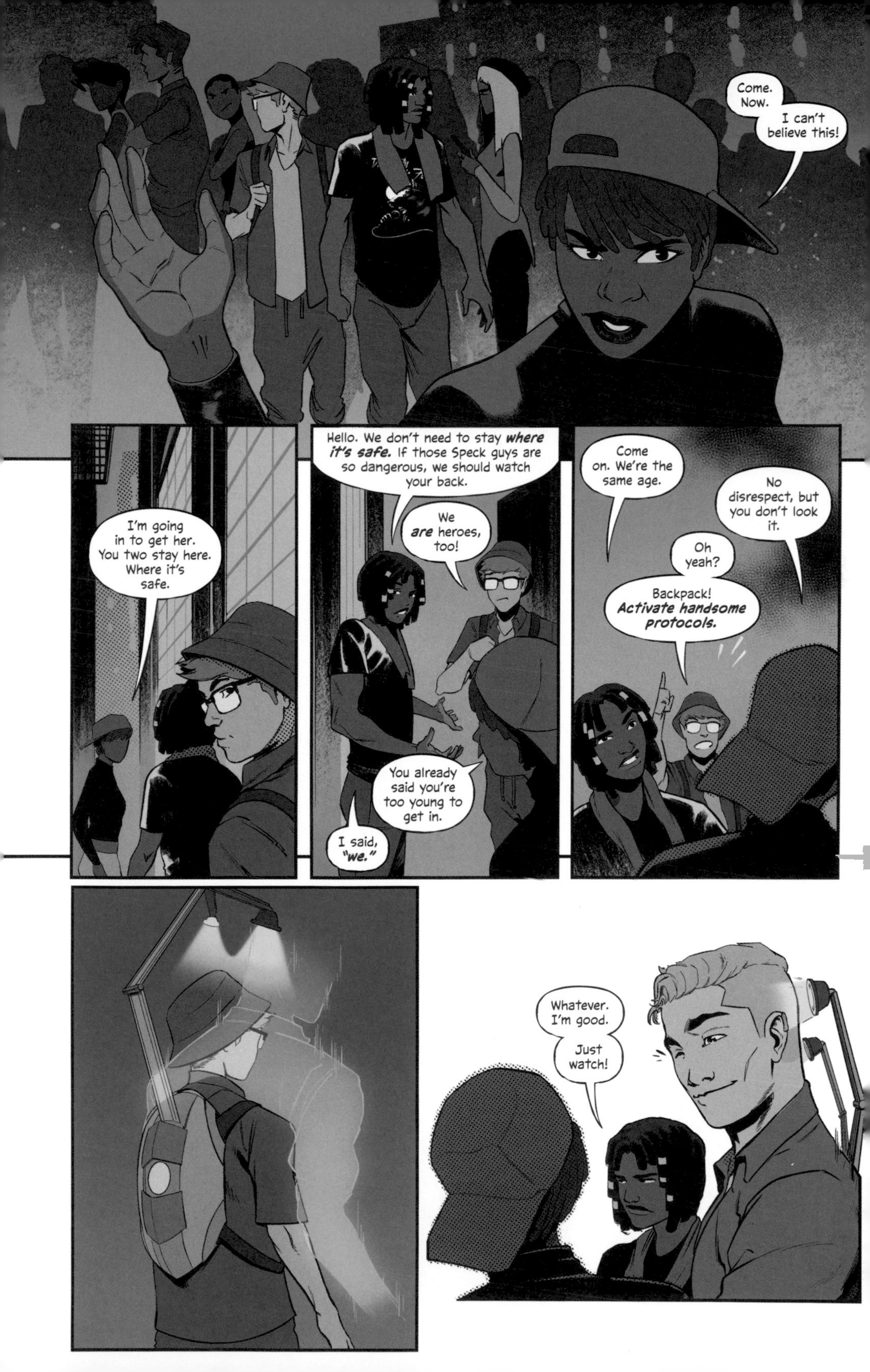
Come. Now.
I can't believe this!
I'm going in to get her. You two stay here. Where it's safe.
Hello. We don't need to stay *where it's safe.* If those Speck guys are so dangerous, we should watch your back.
We *are* heroes, too!
You already said you're too young to get in.
I said, *"we."*
Come on. We're the same age.
No disrespect, but you don't look it.
Oh yeah?
Backpack! ***Activate handsome protocols.***
Whatever. I'm good.
Just watch!

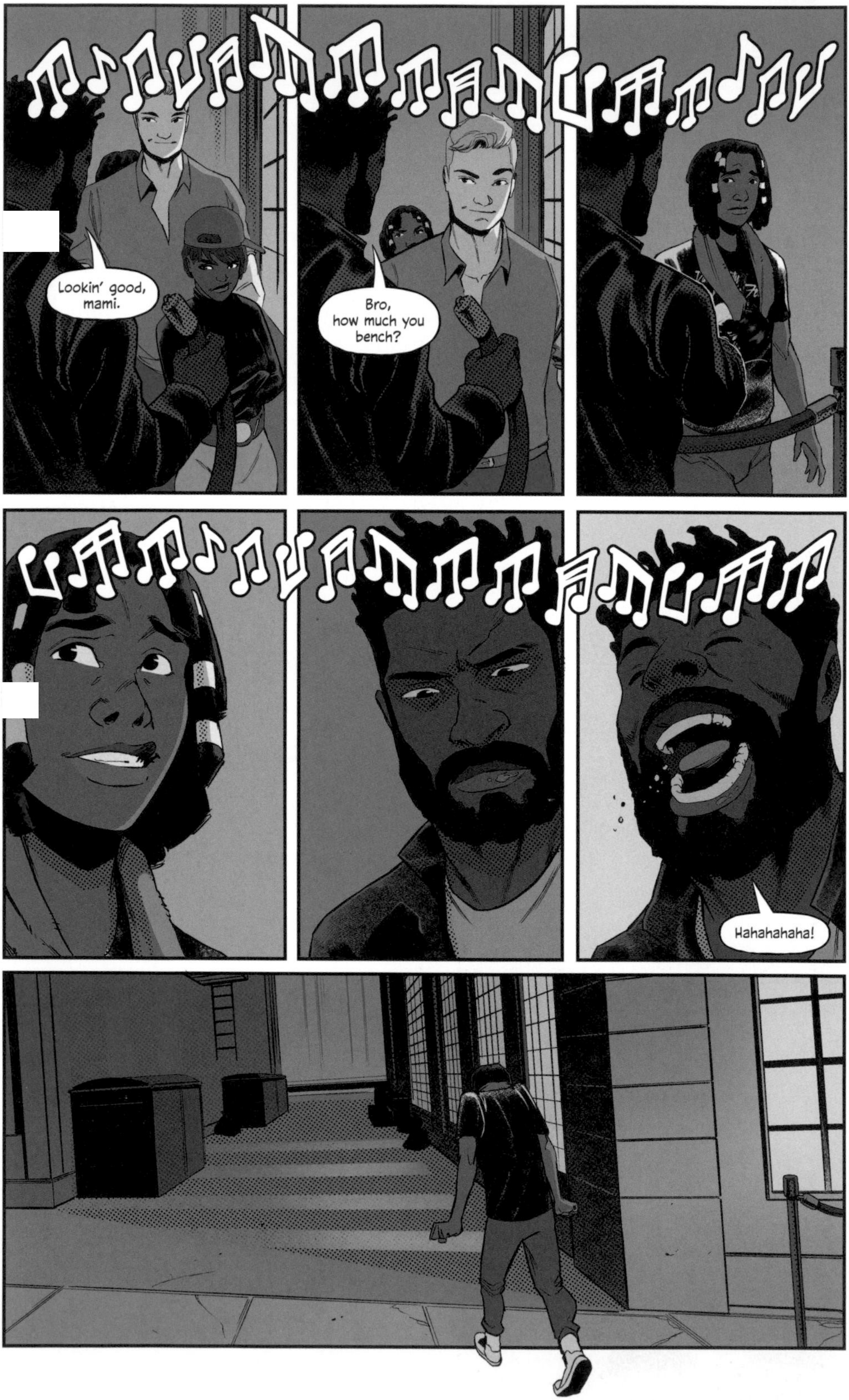
Lookin' good, mami.
Bro, how much you bench?
Hahahahaha!

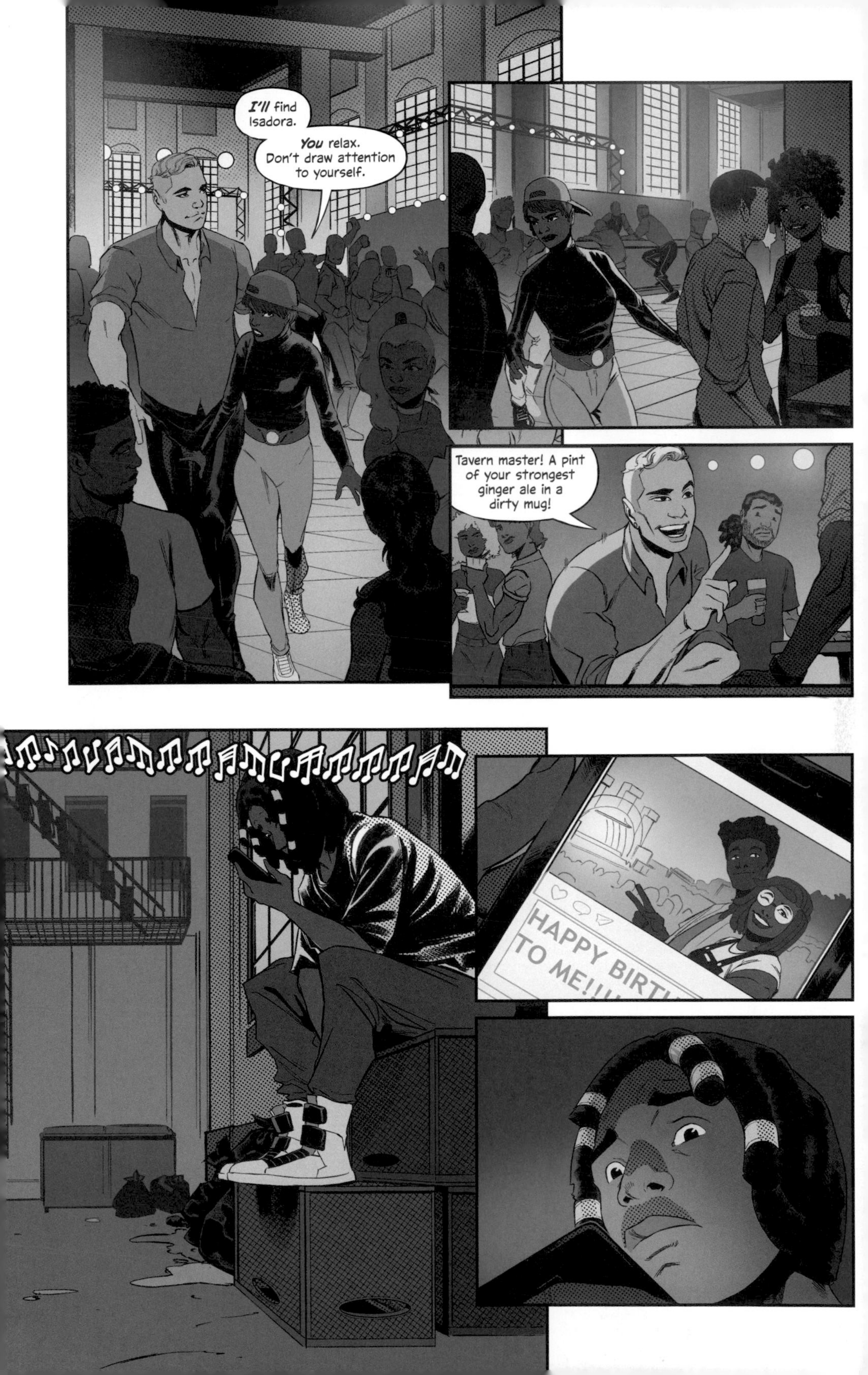

I'll find Isadora.
You relax. Don't draw attention to yourself.
Tavern master! A pint of your strongest ginger ale in a dirty mug!
HAPPY BIRTH
TO ME!!!

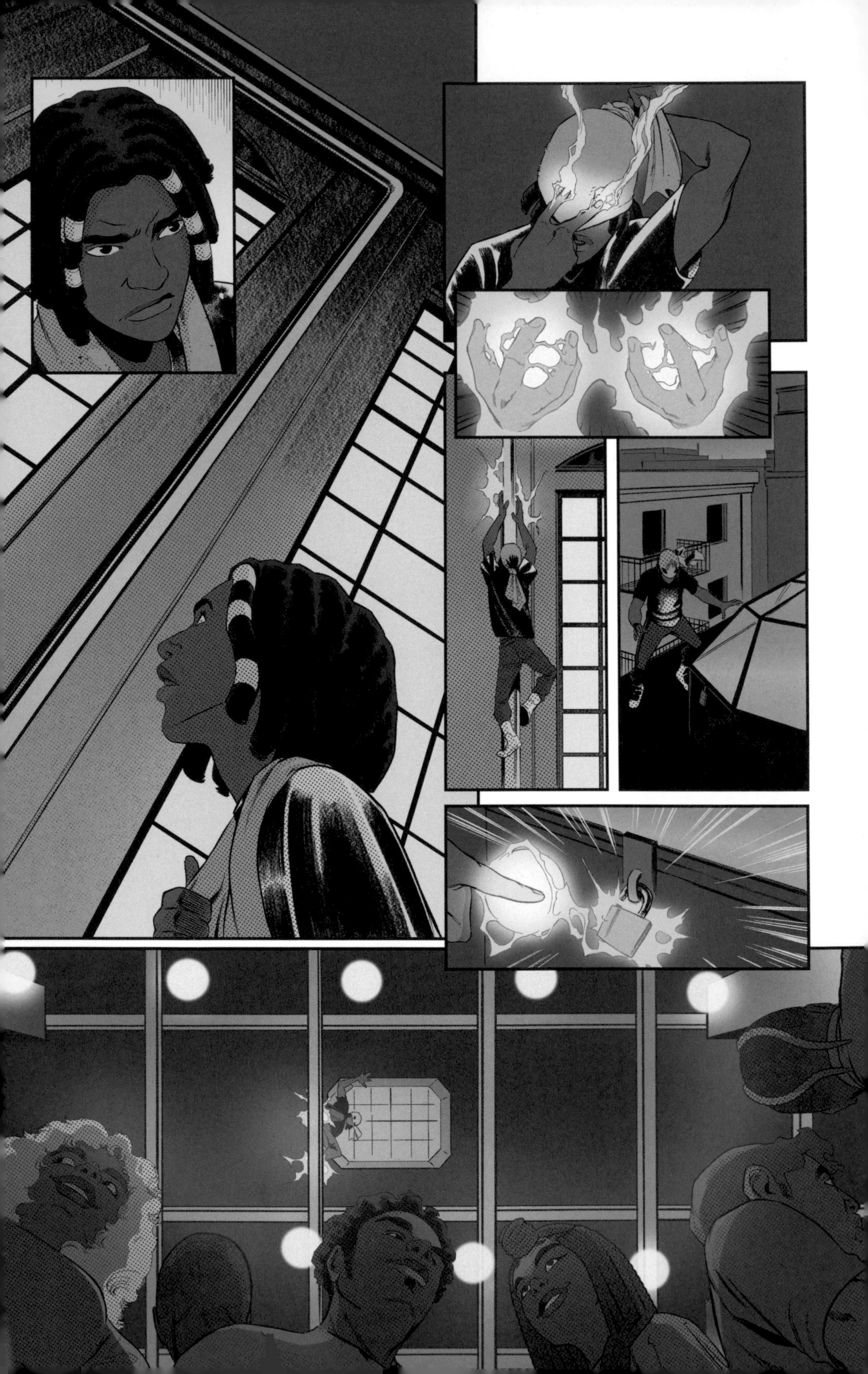

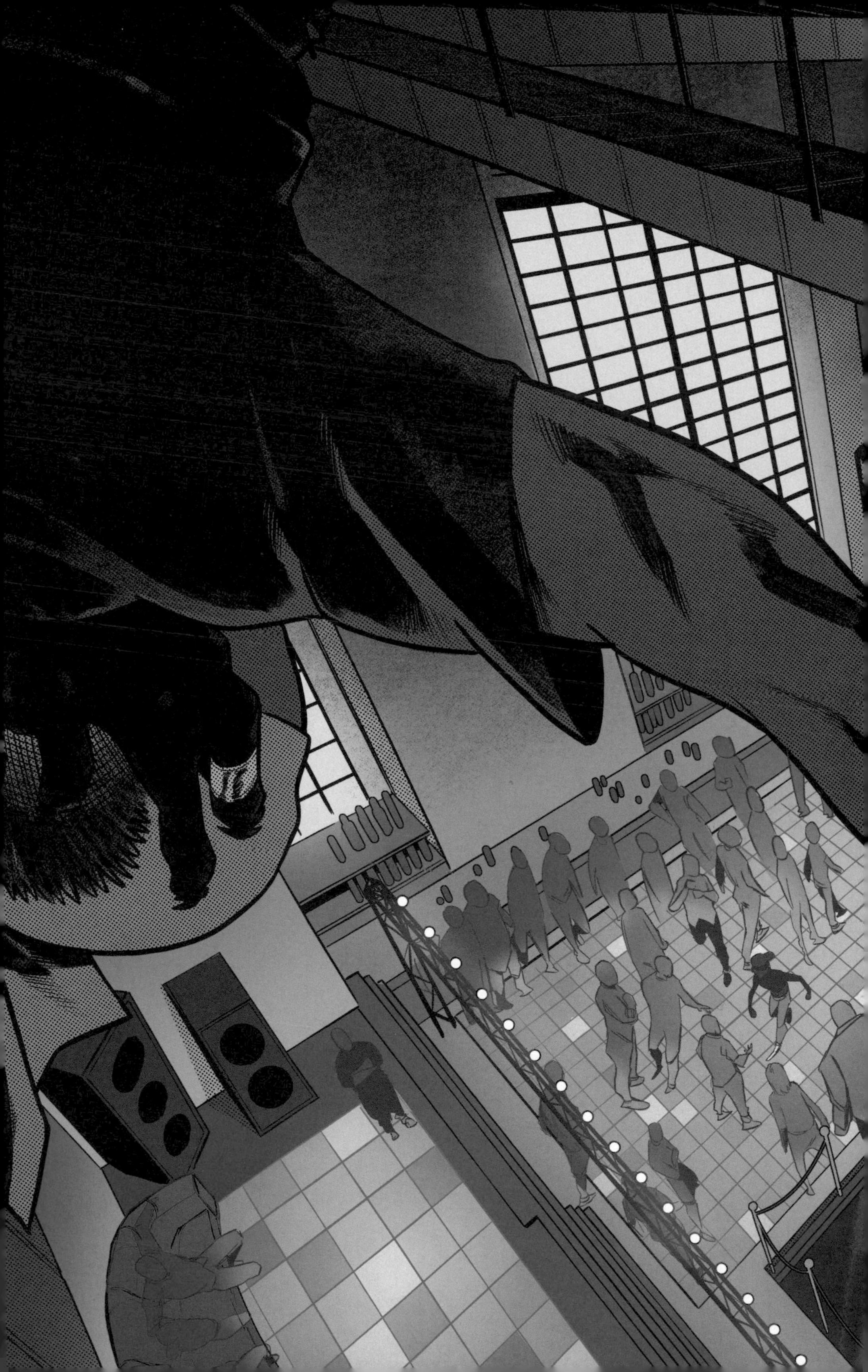

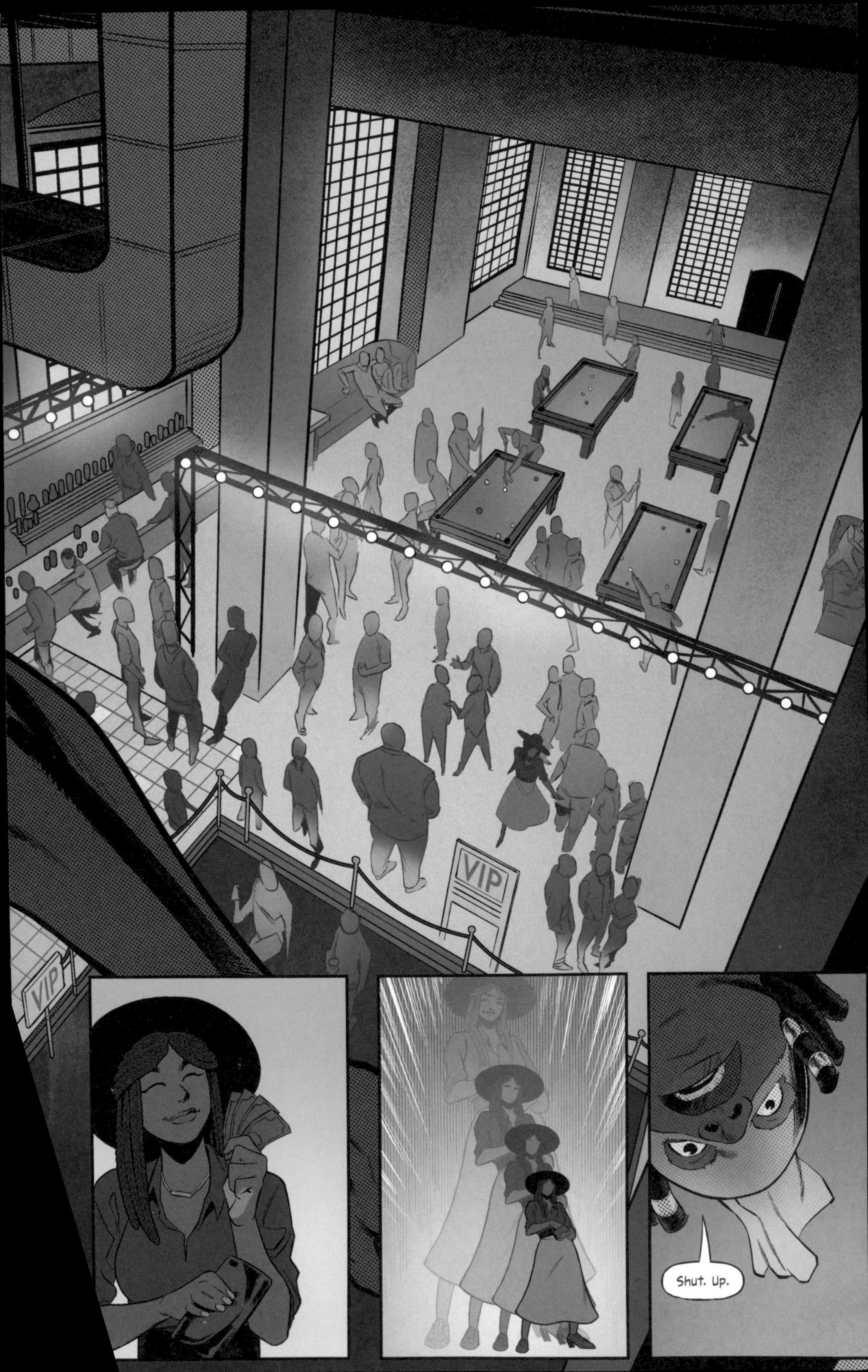
VIP
VIP
Shut. Up.

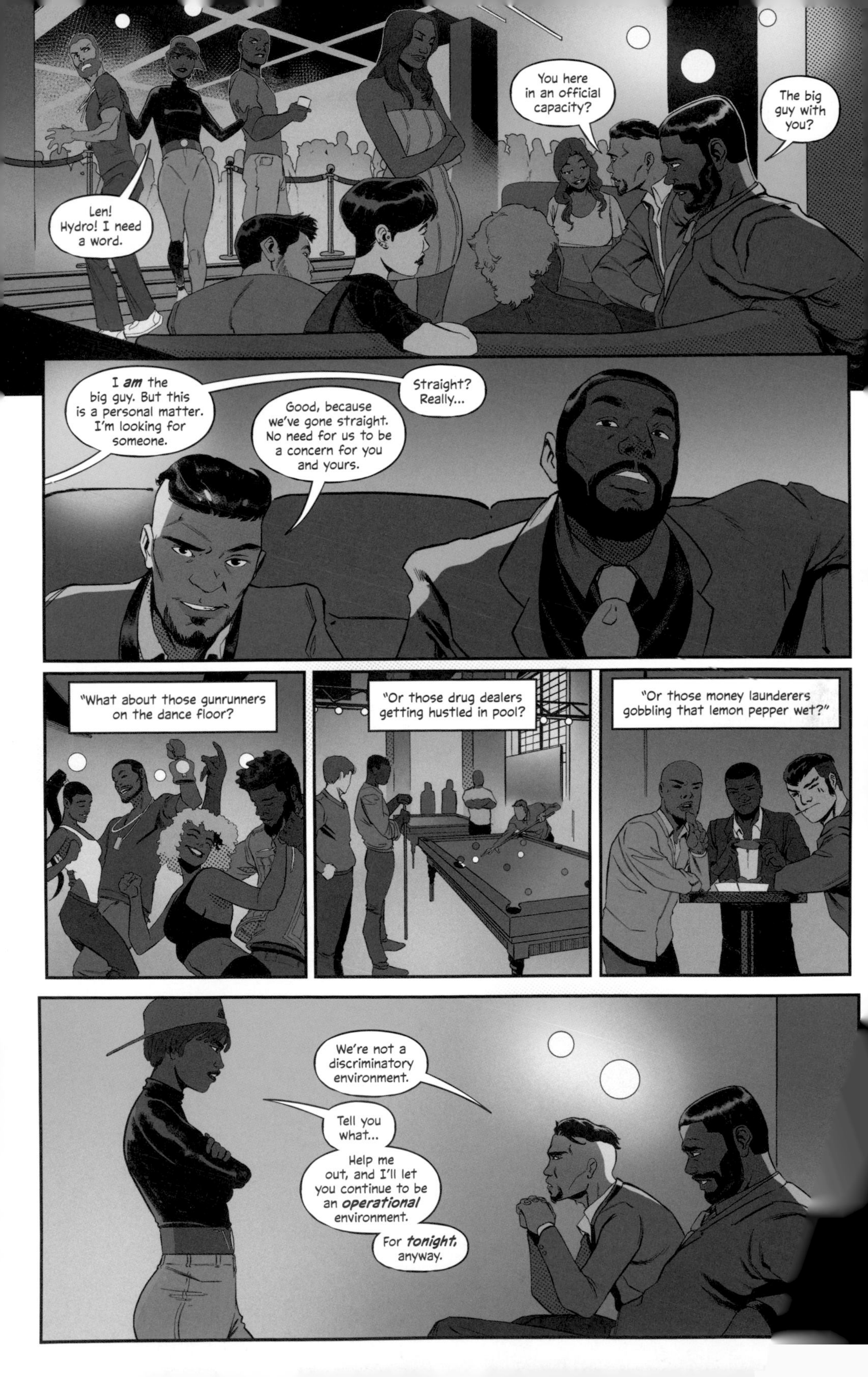
Len! Hydro! I need a word.
You here in an official capacity?
The big guy with you?
I *am* the big guy. But this is a personal matter. I'm looking for someone.
Good, because we've gone straight. No need for us to be a concern for you and yours.
Straight? Really...
"What about those gunrunners on the dance floor?
"Or those drug dealers getting hustled in pool?
"Or those money launderers gobbling that lemon pepper wet?"
We're not a discriminatory environment.
Tell you what...
Help me out, and I'll let you continue to be an *operational* environment.
For *tonight,* anyway.

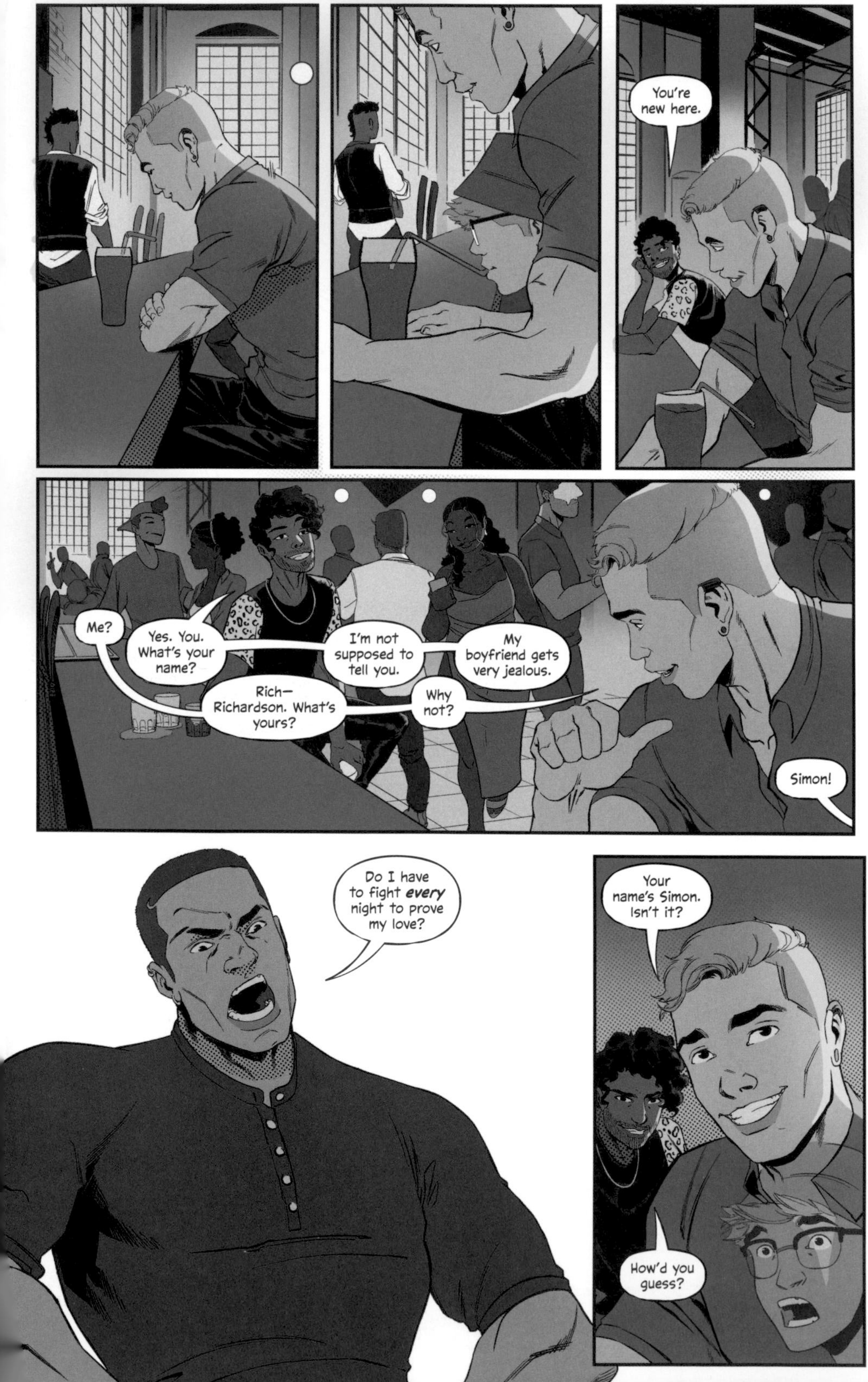
You're new here.
Me?
Yes. You. What's your name?
Rich— Richardson. What's yours?
I'm not supposed to tell you.
Why not?
My boyfriend gets very jealous.
Simon!
Do I have to fight *every* night to prove my love?
Your name's Simon. Isn't it?
How'd you guess?

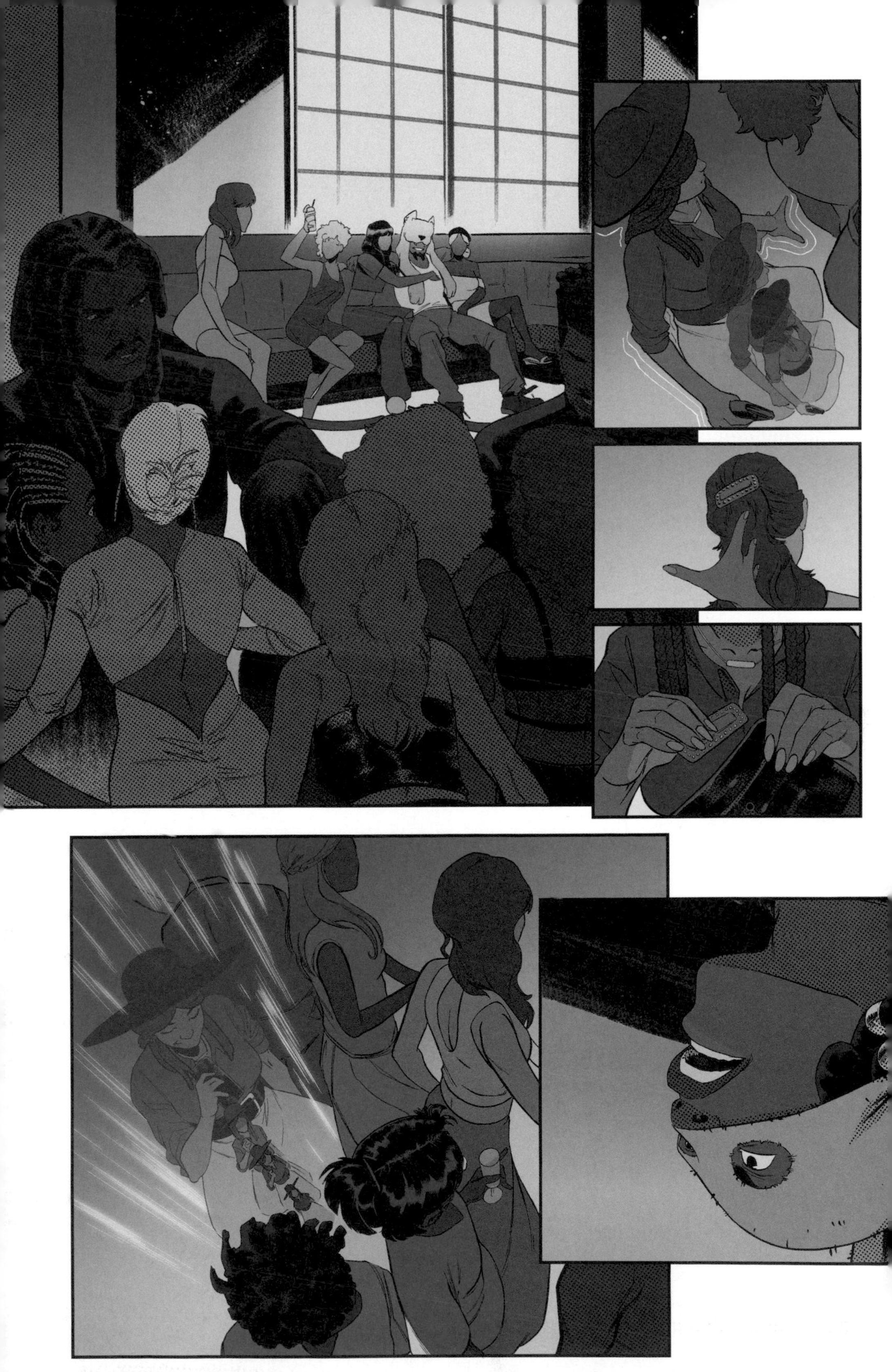

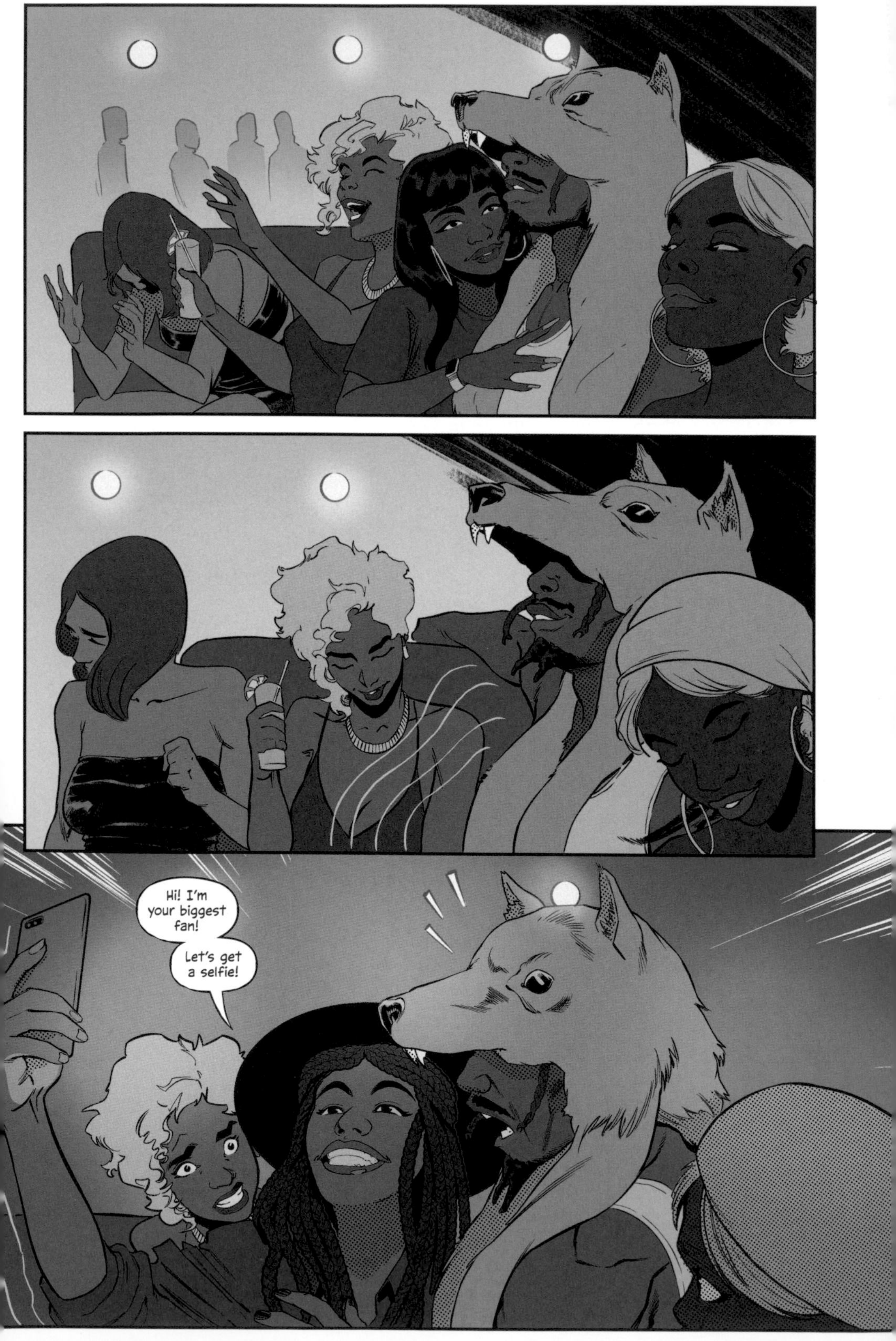
Hi! I'm your biggest fan!
Let's get a selfie!

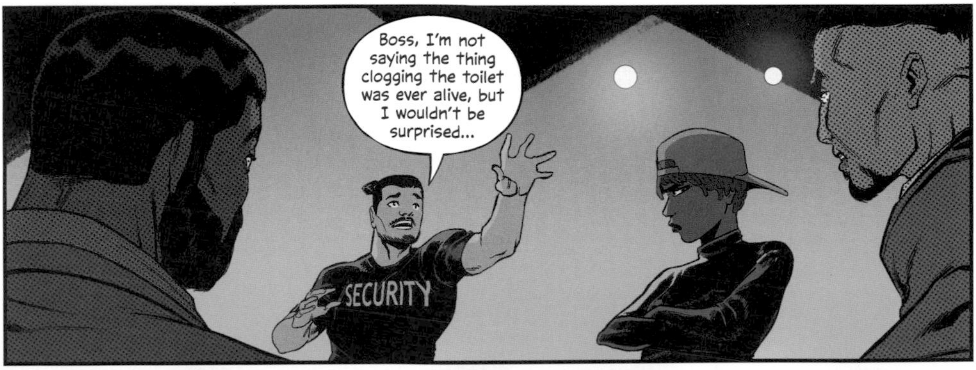
Boss, I'm not saying the thing clogging the toilet was ever alive, but I wouldn't be surprised...
SECURITY

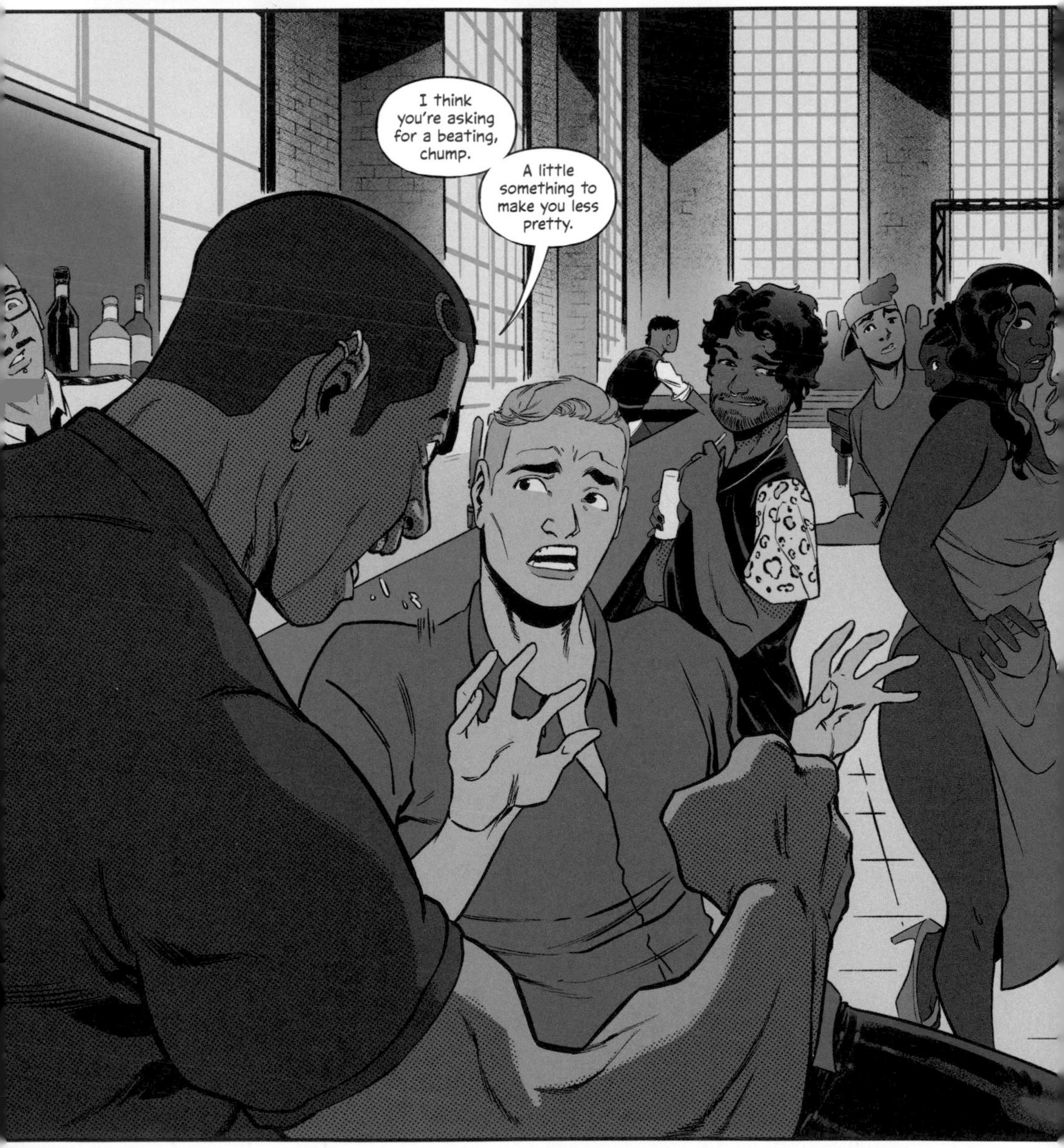
I think you're asking for a beating, chump.
A little something to make you less pretty.

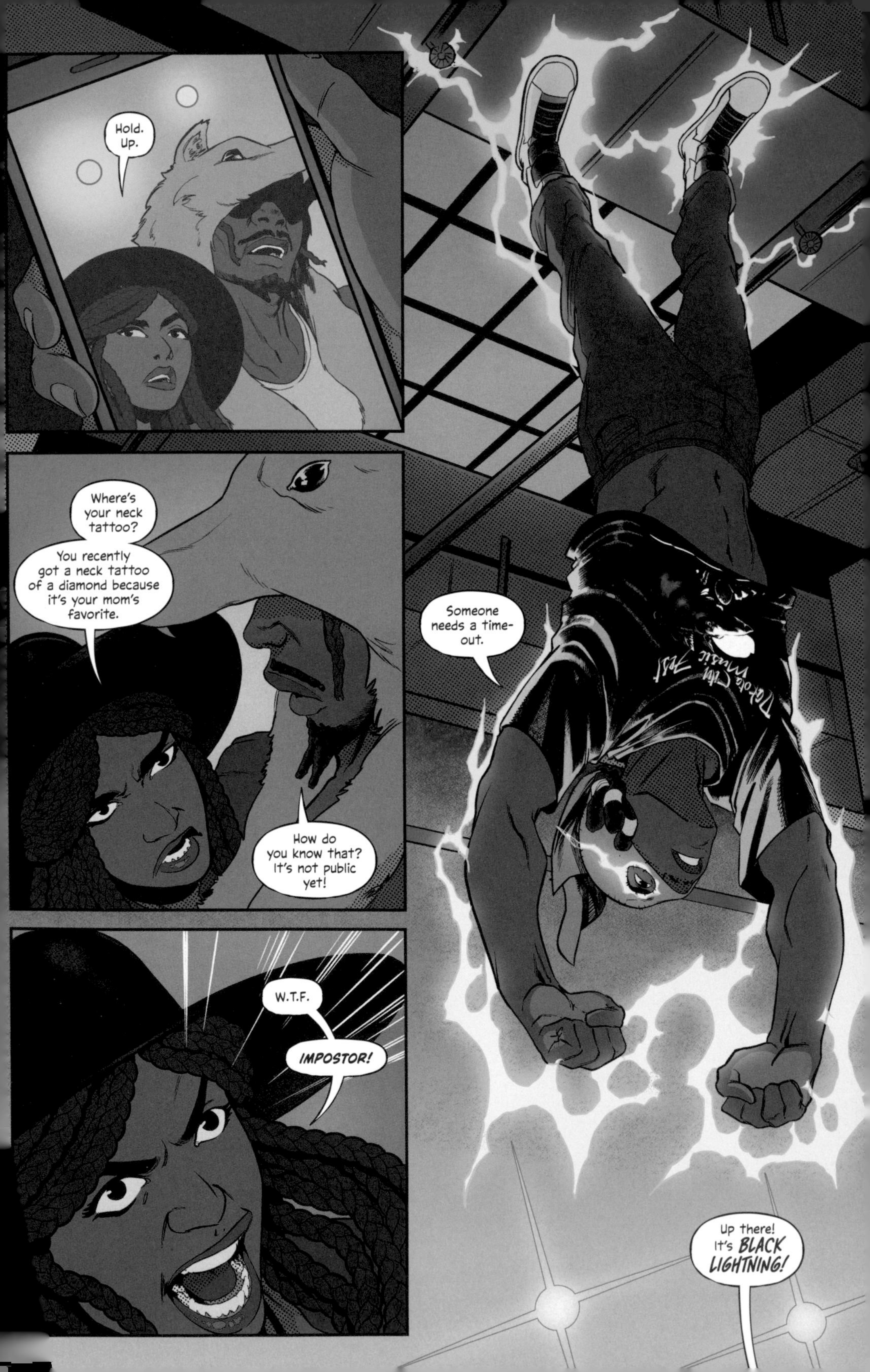

Hold. Up.
Where's your neck tattoo?
You recently got a neck tattoo of a diamond because it's your mom's favorite.
How do you know that? It's not public yet!
W.T.F.
IMPOSTOR!
Someone needs a time-out.
Up there! It's BLACK LIGHTNING!

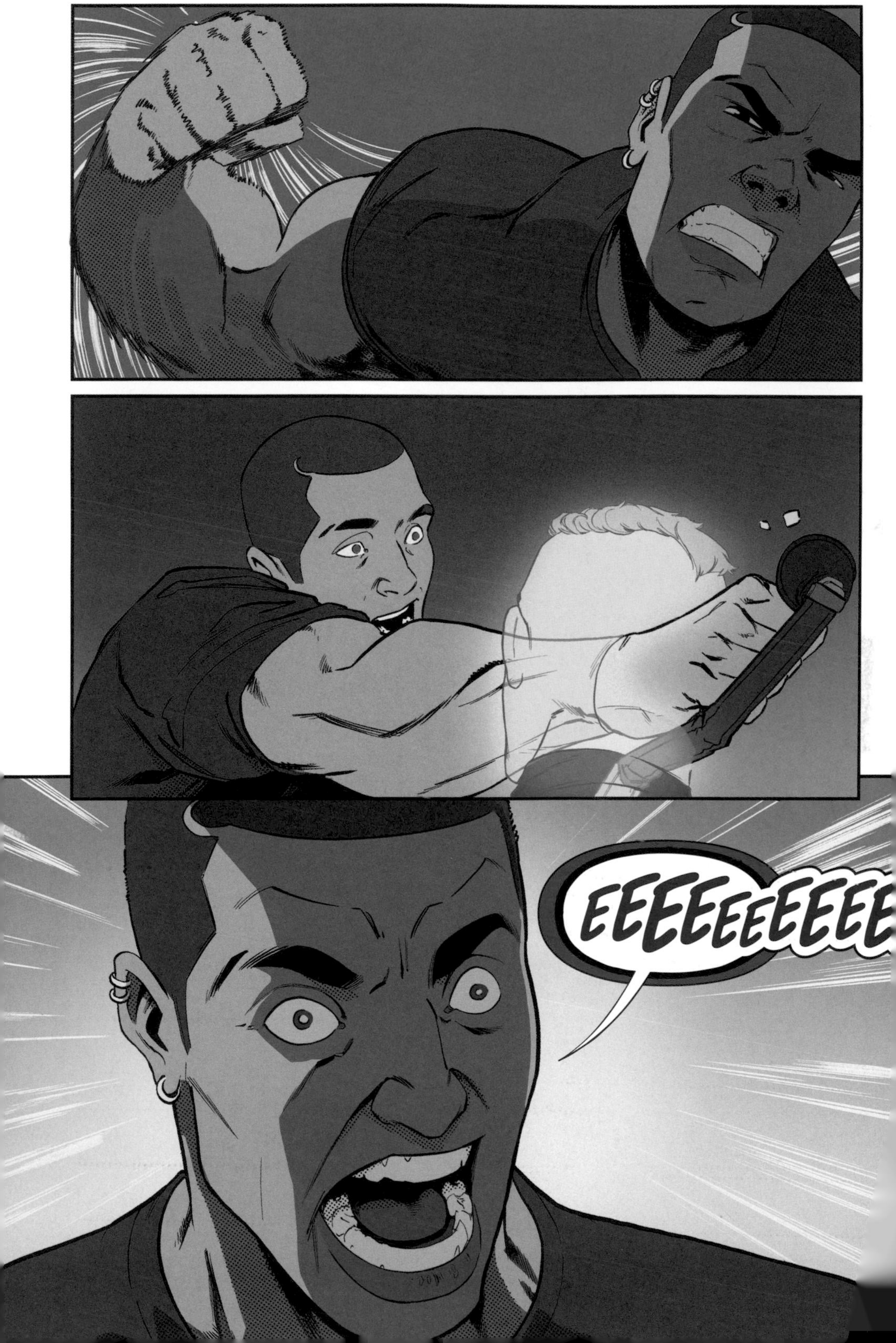
EEEEEEEEEE

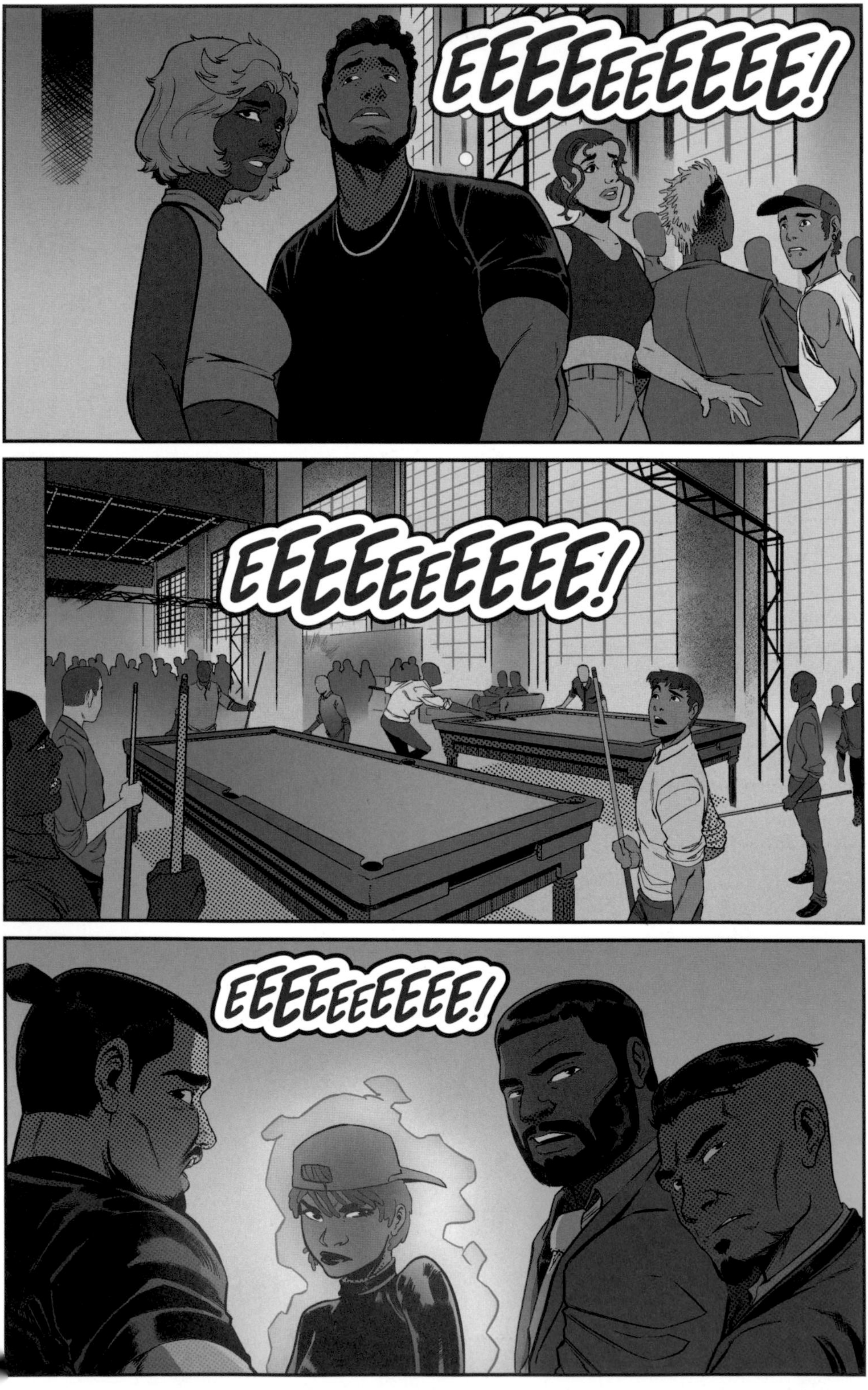
EEEEEEEEEE!
EEEEEEEEEE!
EEEEEEEEEE!

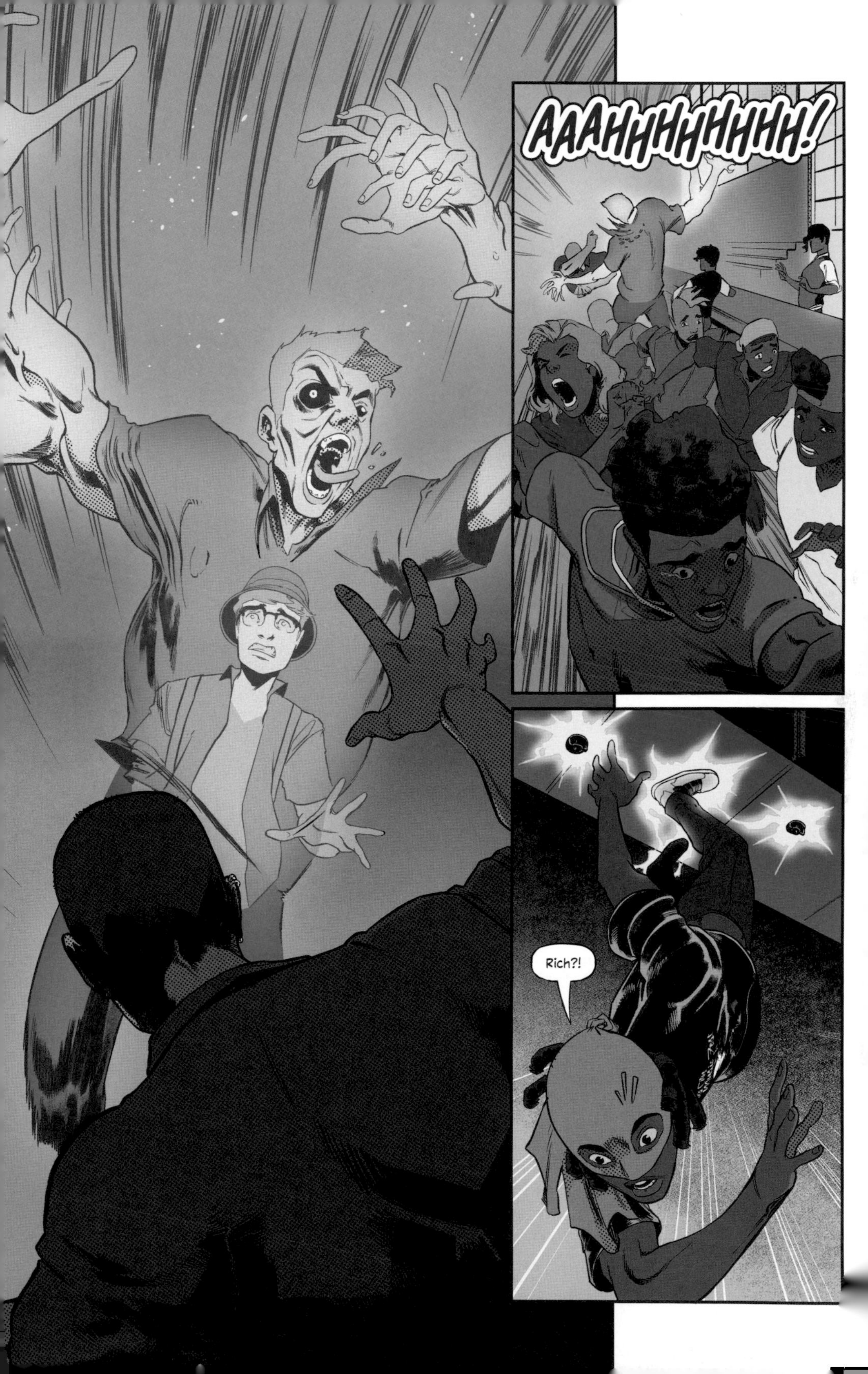
AAAHHHHHHHH!
Rich?!

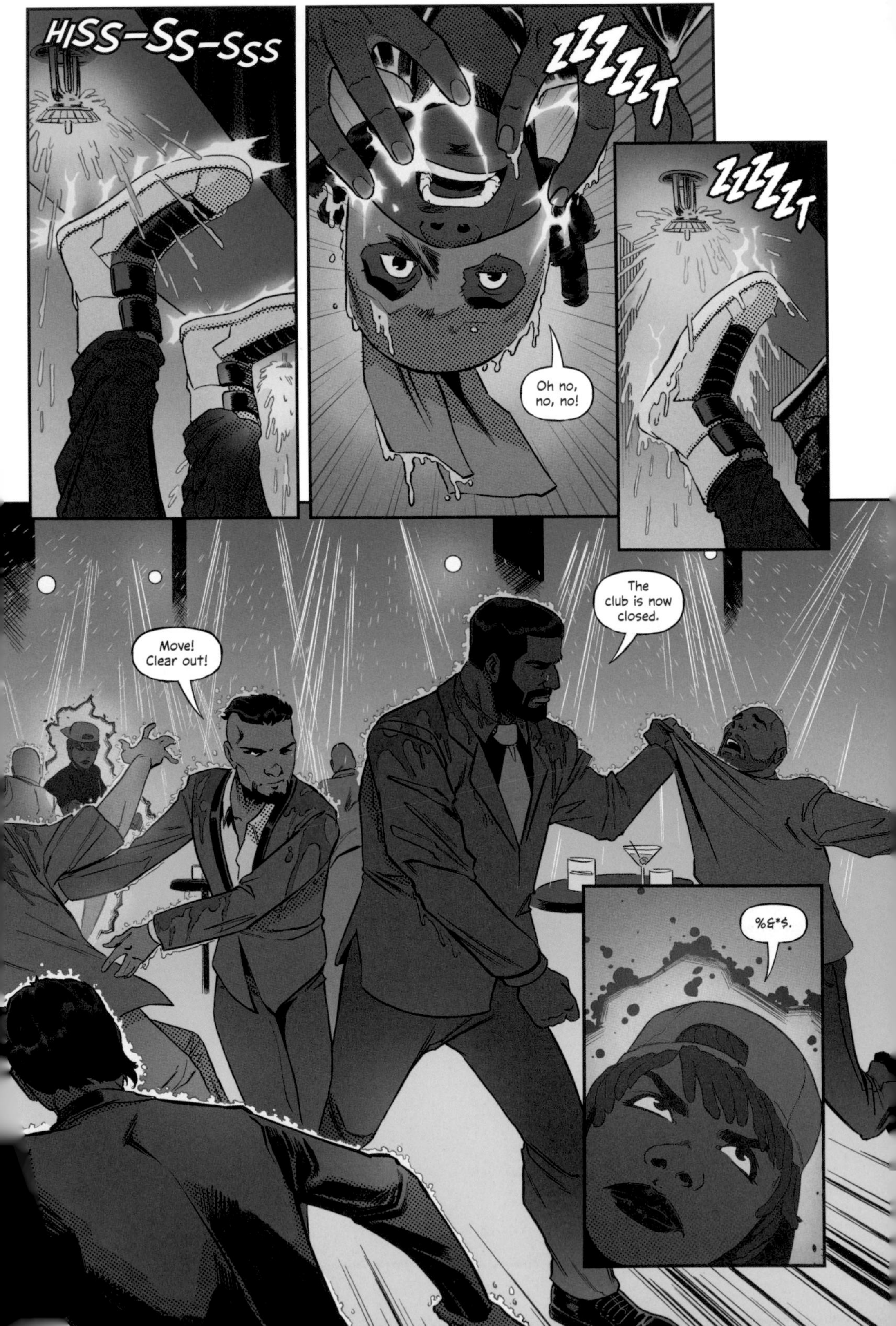
HISS-SS-SSS
ZZZZZZT
Oh no, no, no!
ZZZZZZT
Move! Clear out!
The club is now closed.
%&*$.

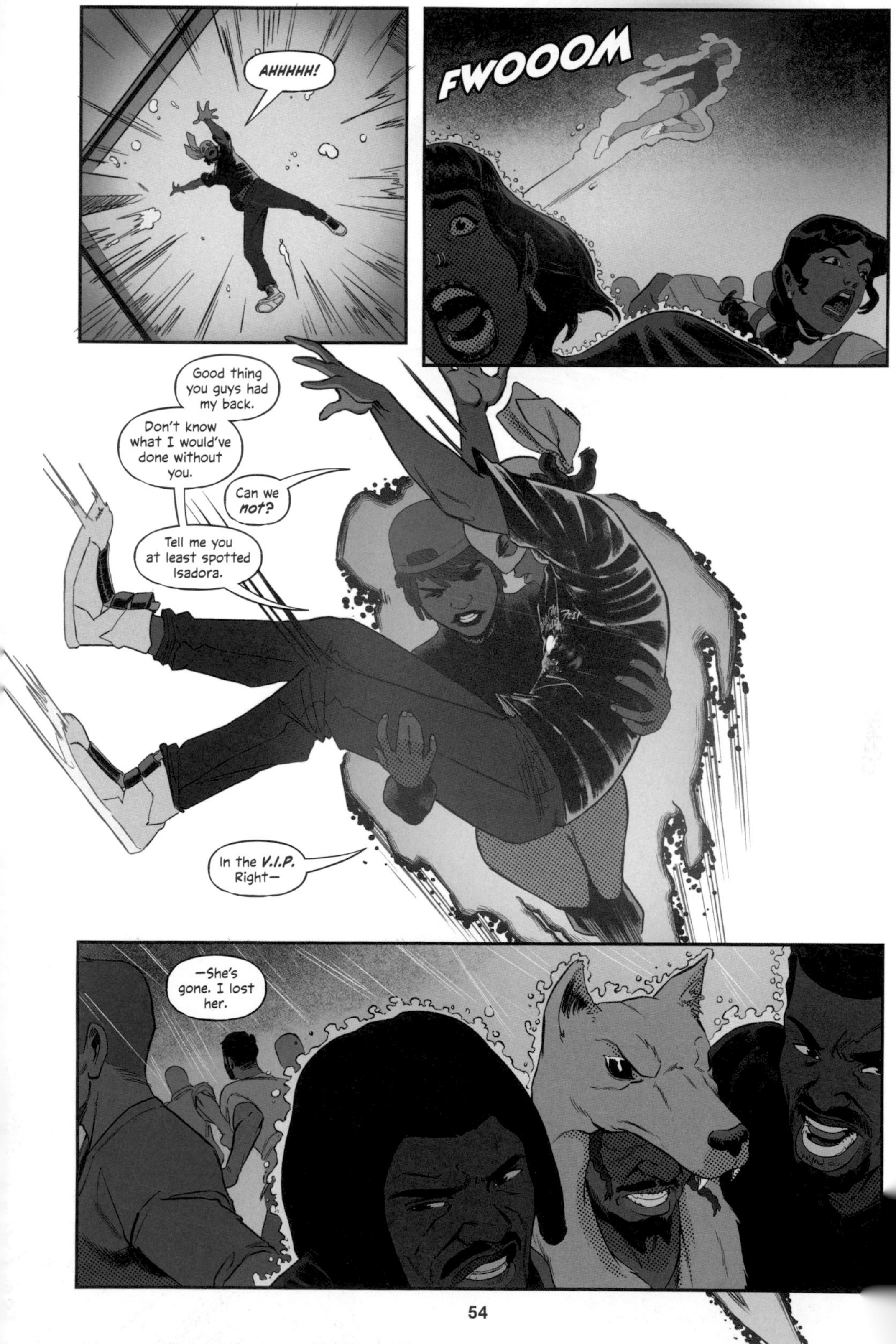
AHHHHH!
FWOOOM
Good thing you guys had my back.
Don't know what I would've done without you.
Can we *not?*
Tell me you at least spotted Isadora.
In the *V.I.P.* Right—
—She's gone. I lost her.

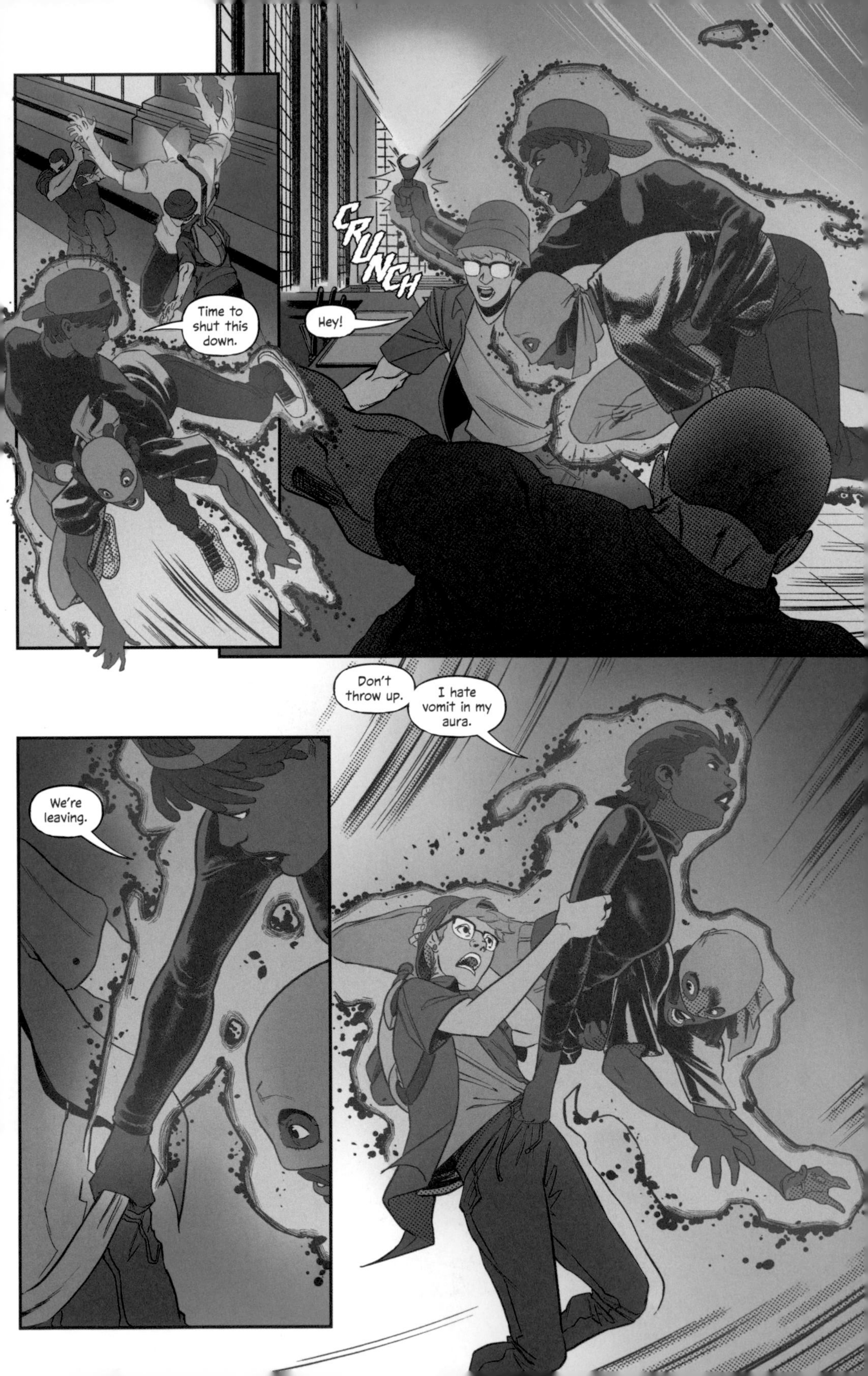
Time to shut this down.
Hey!
CRUNCH
Don't throw up.
I hate vomit in my aura.
We're leaving.

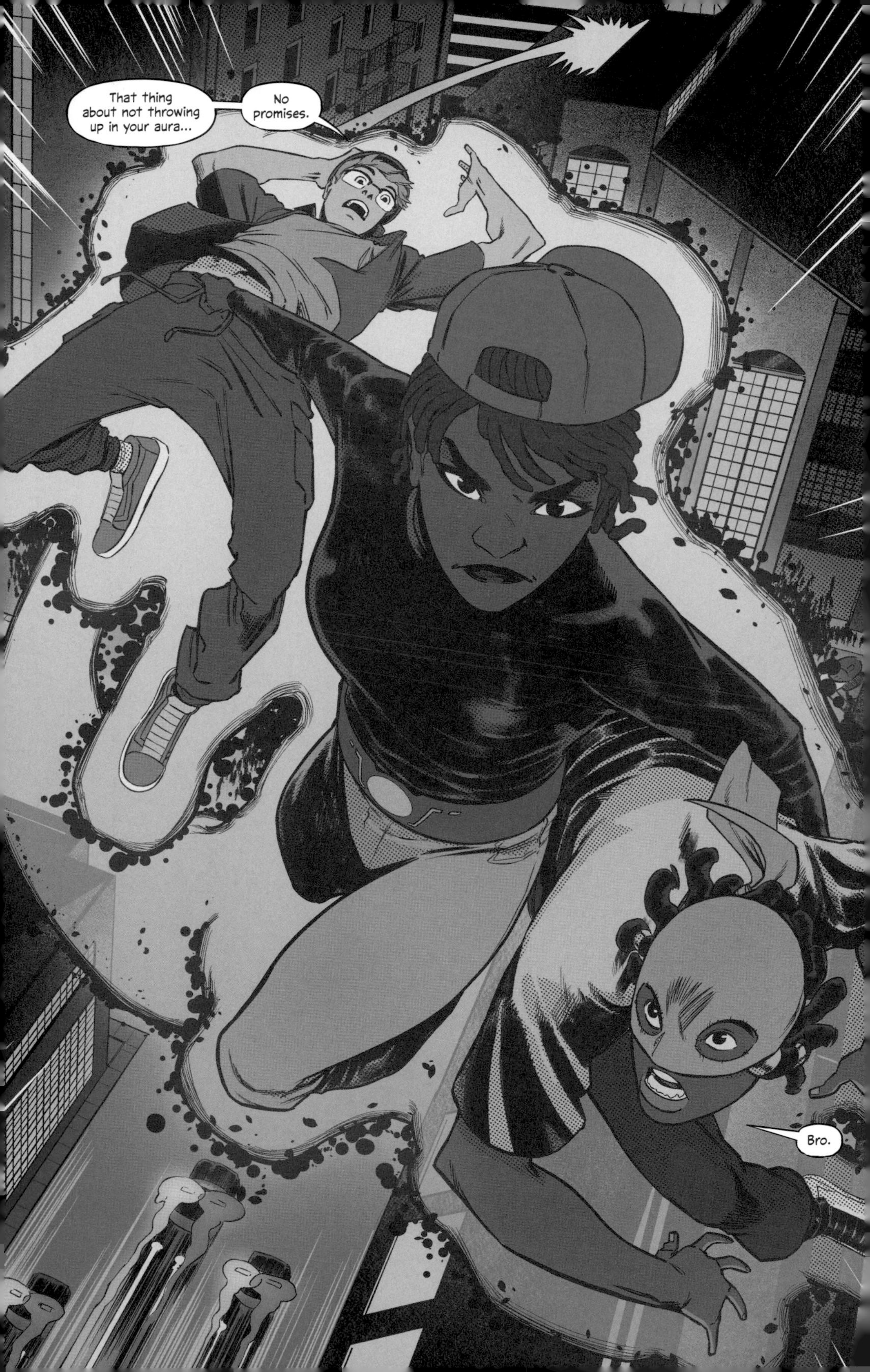
That thing about not throwing up in your aura...
No promises.
Bro.

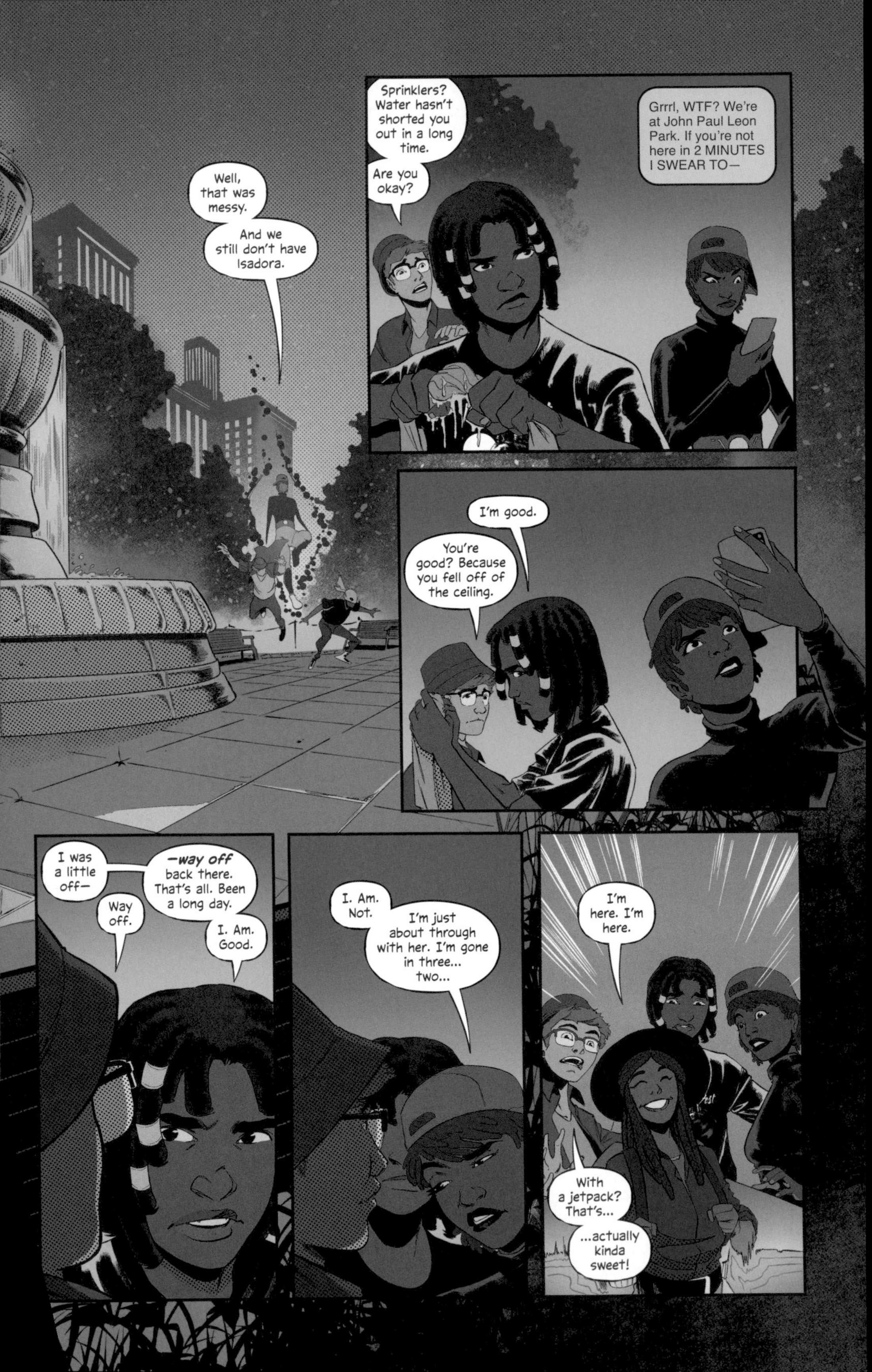

Well, that was messy.
And we still don't have Isadora.
Sprinklers? Water hasn't shorted you out in a long time.
Are you okay?
Grrrl, WTF? We're at John Paul Leon Park. If you're not here in 2 MINUTES I SWEAR TO—
I'm good.
You're good? Because you fell off of the ceiling.
I was a little off—
—way off back there. That's all. Been a long day.
Way off.
I. Am. Good.
I. Am. Not.
I'm just about through with her. I'm gone in three... two...
I'm here. I'm here.
With a jetpack? That's...
...actually kinda sweet!

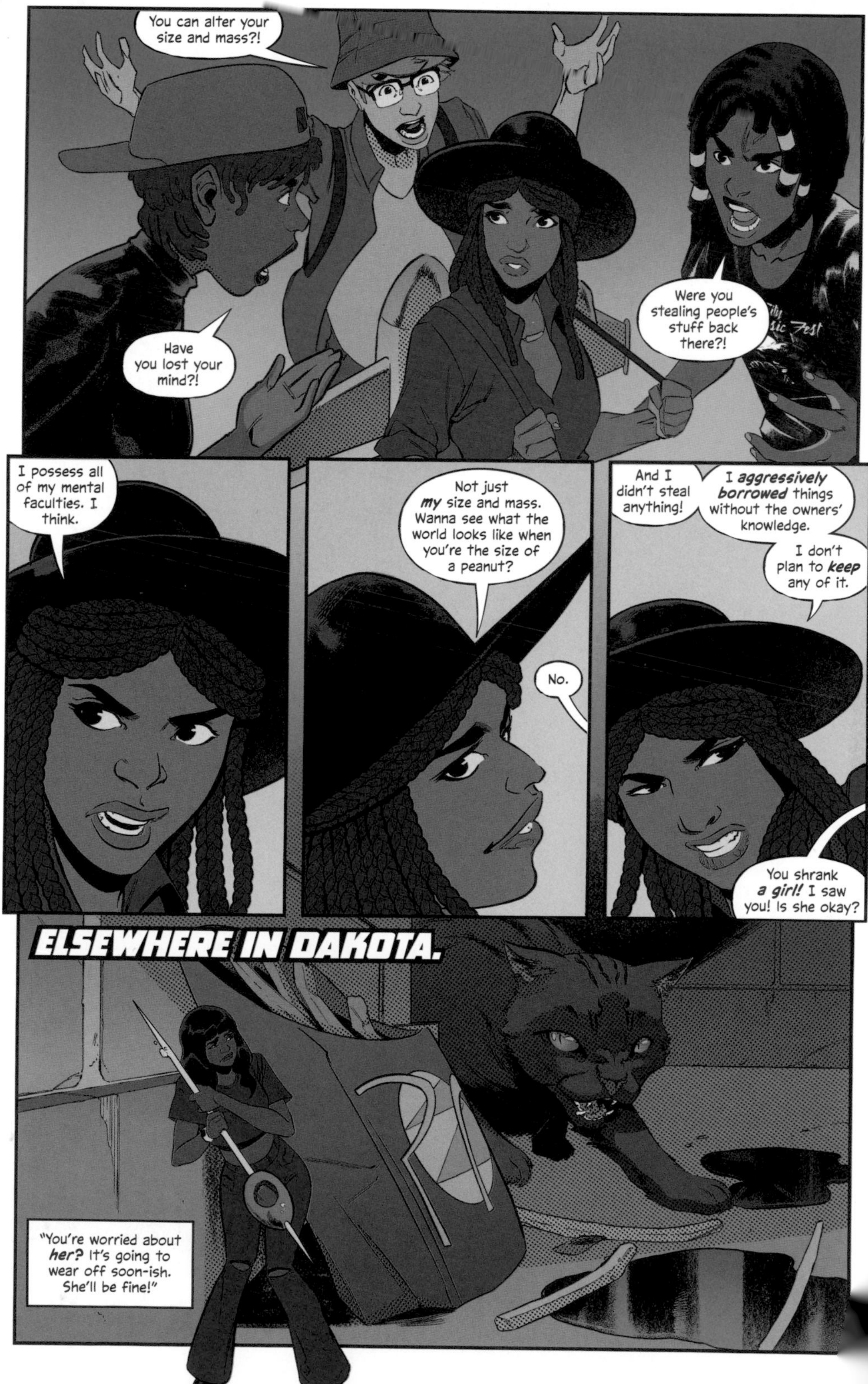
You can alter your size and mass?!
Have you lost your mind?!
Were you stealing people's stuff back there?!
I possess all of my mental faculties. I think.
Not just *my* size and mass. Wanna see what the world looks like when you're the size of a peanut?
No.
And I didn't steal anything!
I ***aggressively borrowed*** things without the owners' knowledge.
I don't plan to ***keep*** any of it.
You shrank ***a girl!*** I saw you! Is she okay?
ELSEWHERE IN DAKOTA.
"You're worried about ***her?*** It's going to wear off soon-ish. She'll be fine!"

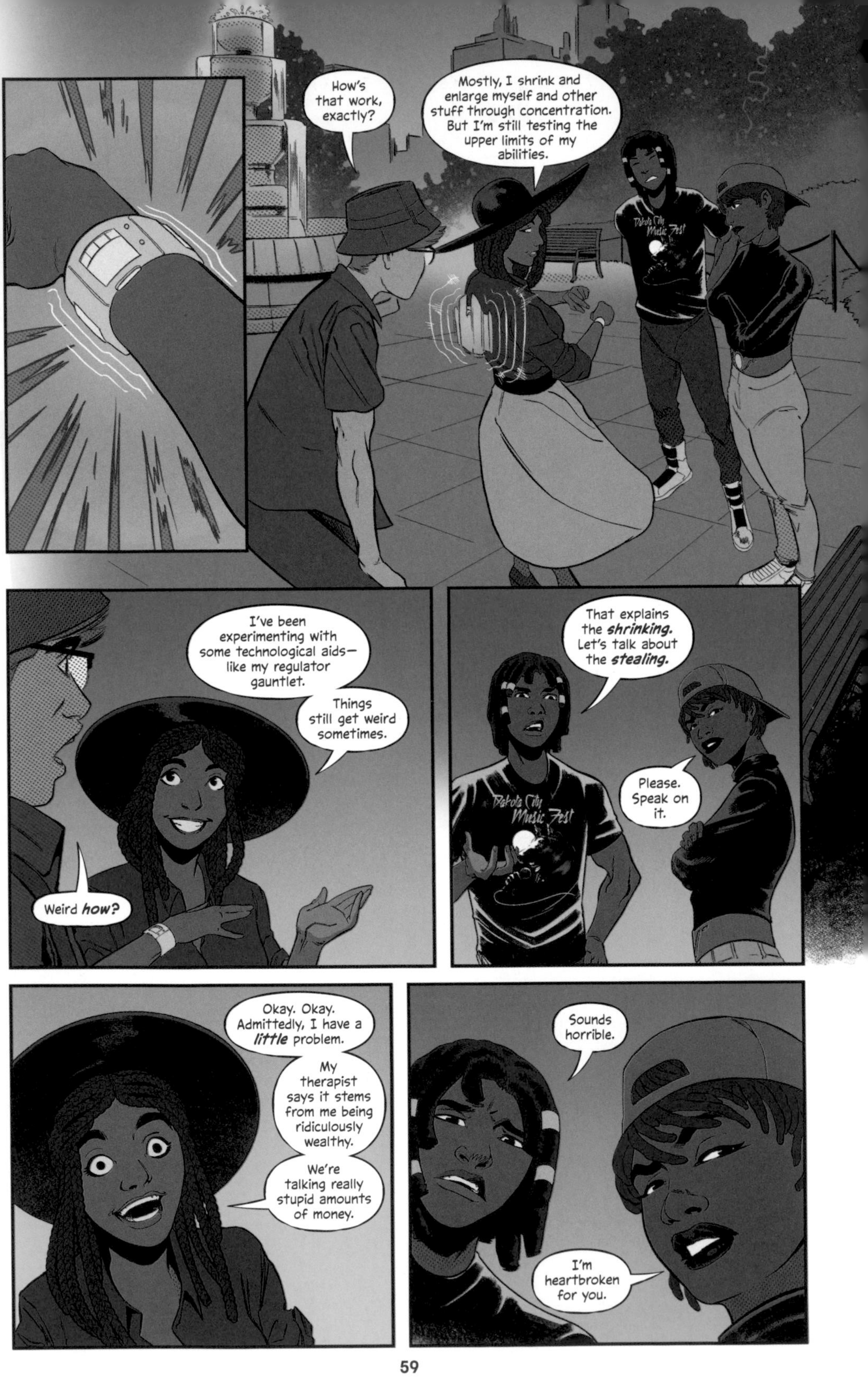
How's that work, exactly?
Mostly, I shrink and enlarge myself and other stuff through concentration. But I'm still testing the upper limits of my abilities.
I've been experimenting with some technological aids—like my regulator gauntlet.
Things still get weird sometimes.
Weird *how?*
That explains the ***shrinking.*** Let's talk about the ***stealing.***
Please. Speak on it.
Dakota City Music Fest
Okay. Okay. Admittedly, I have a ***little*** problem.
My therapist says it stems from me being ridiculously wealthy.
We're talking really stupid amounts of money.
Sounds horrible.
I'm heartbroken for you.

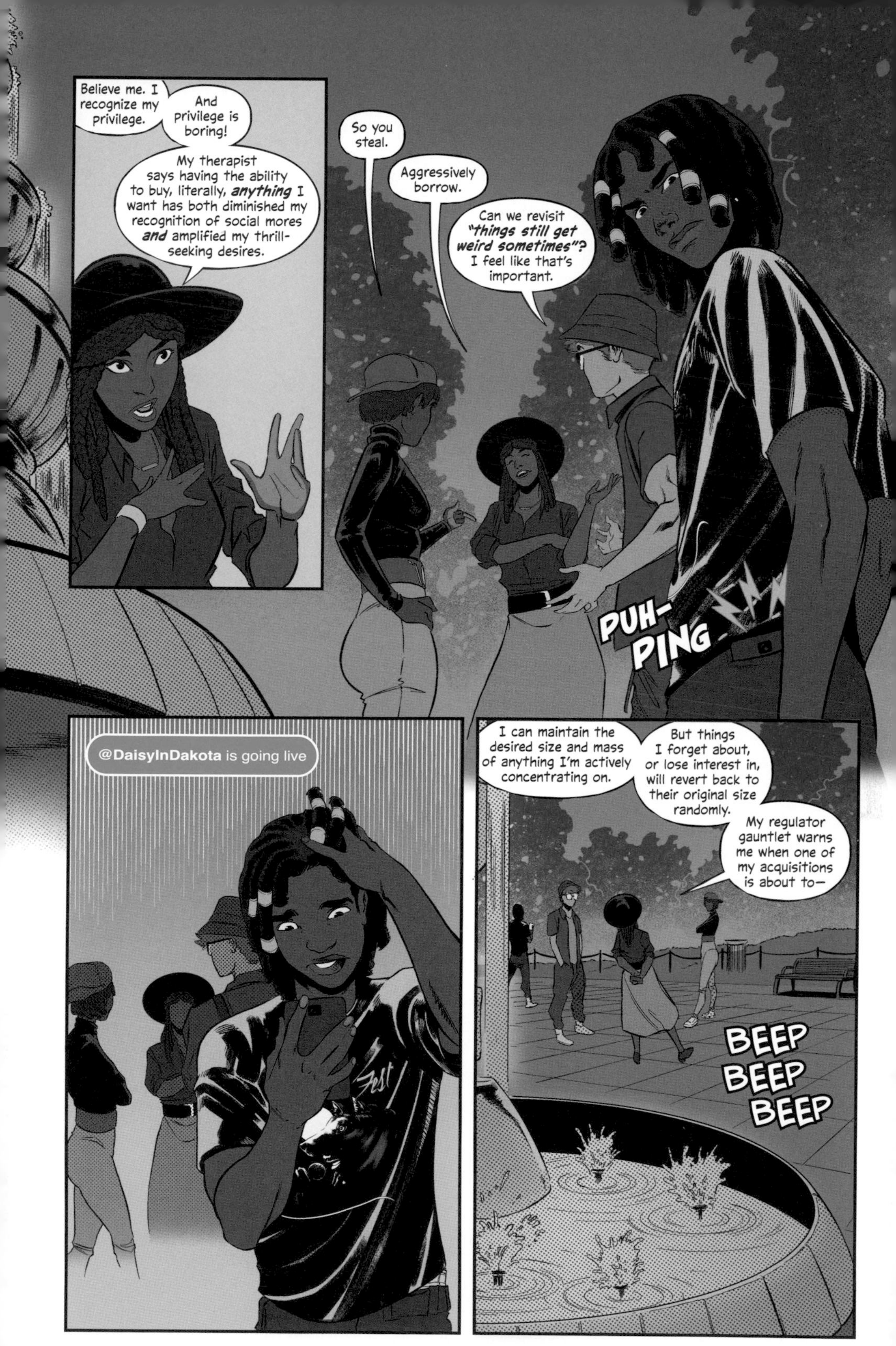
Believe me. I recognize my privilege.
And privilege is boring!
My therapist says having the ability to buy, literally, *anything* I want has both diminished my recognition of social mores *and* amplified my thrill-seeking desires.
So you steal.
Aggressively borrow.
Can we revisit *"things still get weird sometimes"*? I feel like that's important.
PUH-PING
@DaisyInDakota is going live
I can maintain the desired size and mass of anything I'm actively concentrating on.
But things I forget about, or lose interest in, will revert back to their original size randomly.
My regulator gauntlet warns me when one of my acquisitions is about to—
BEEP BEEP BEEP

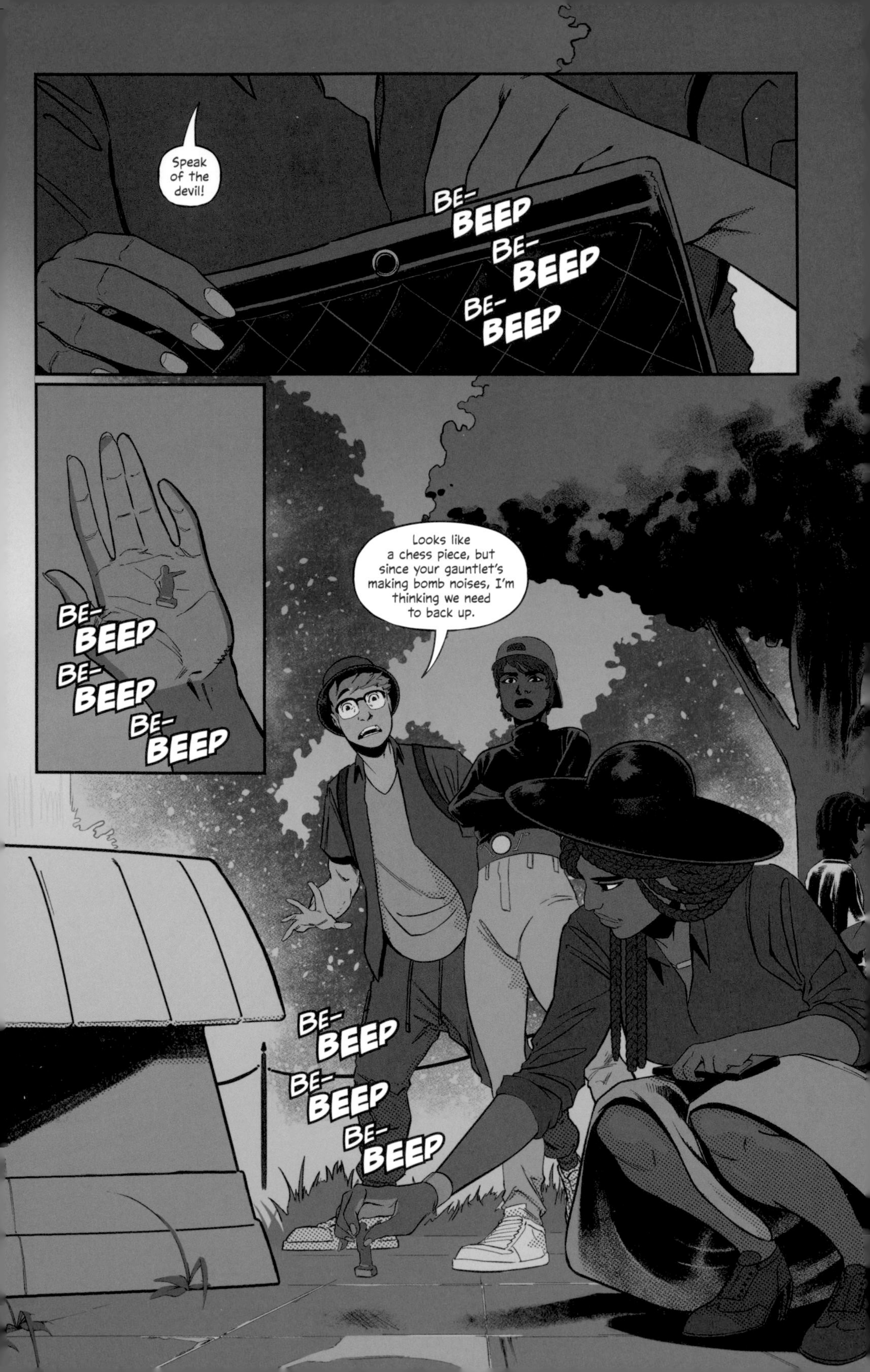
Speak of the devil!
BE-BEEP BE-BEEP BE-BEEP
BE-BEEP BE-BEEP BE-BEEP
Looks like a chess piece, but since your gauntlet's making bomb noises, I'm thinking we need to back up.
BE-BEEP BE-BEEP BE-BEEP

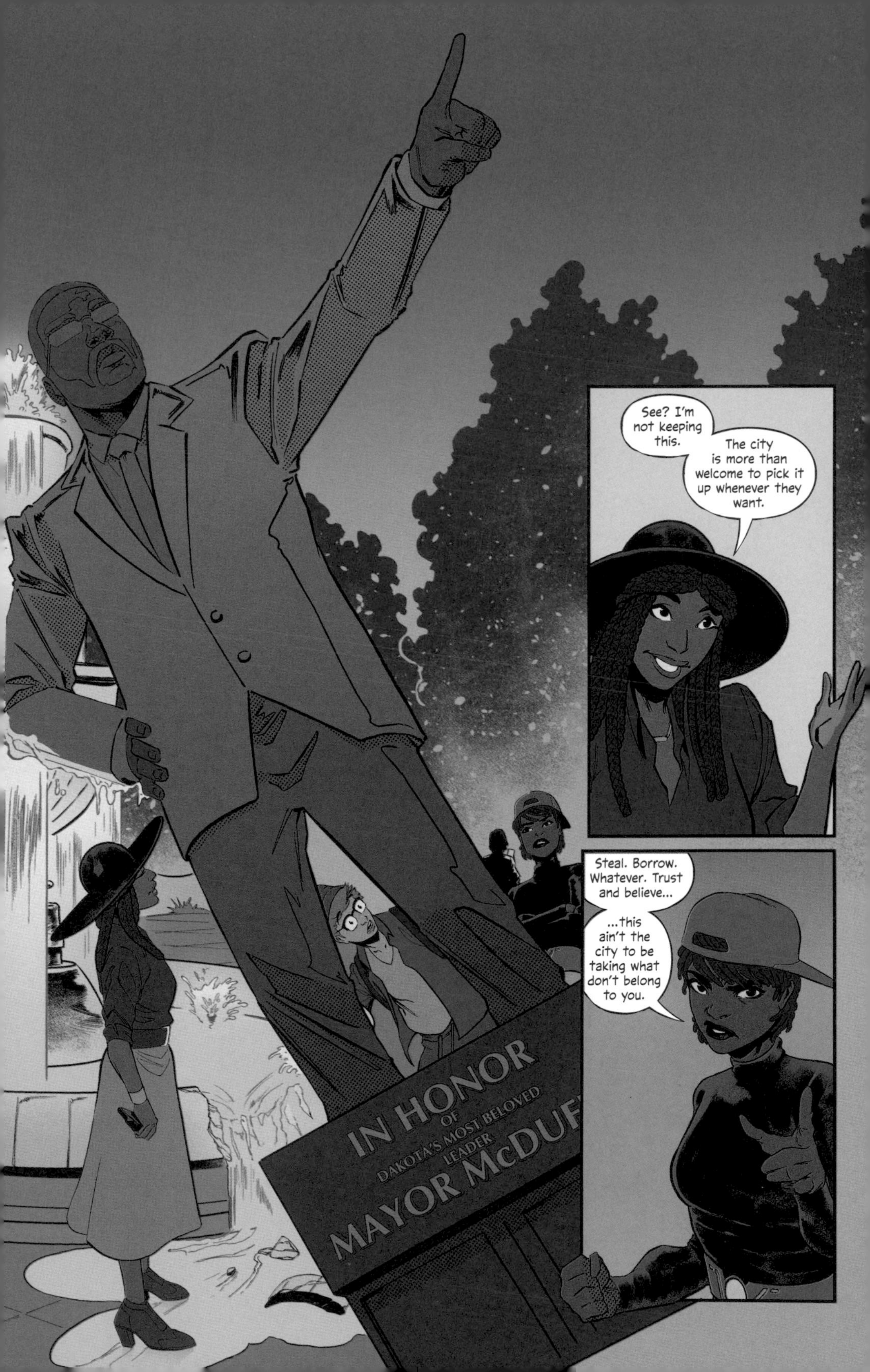
IN HONOR
OF
DAKOTA'S MOST BELOVED
LEADER
MAYOR McDUF
See? I'm not keeping this.
The city is more than welcome to pick it up whenever they want.
Steal. Borrow. Whatever. Trust and believe...
...this ain't the city to be taking what don't belong to you.

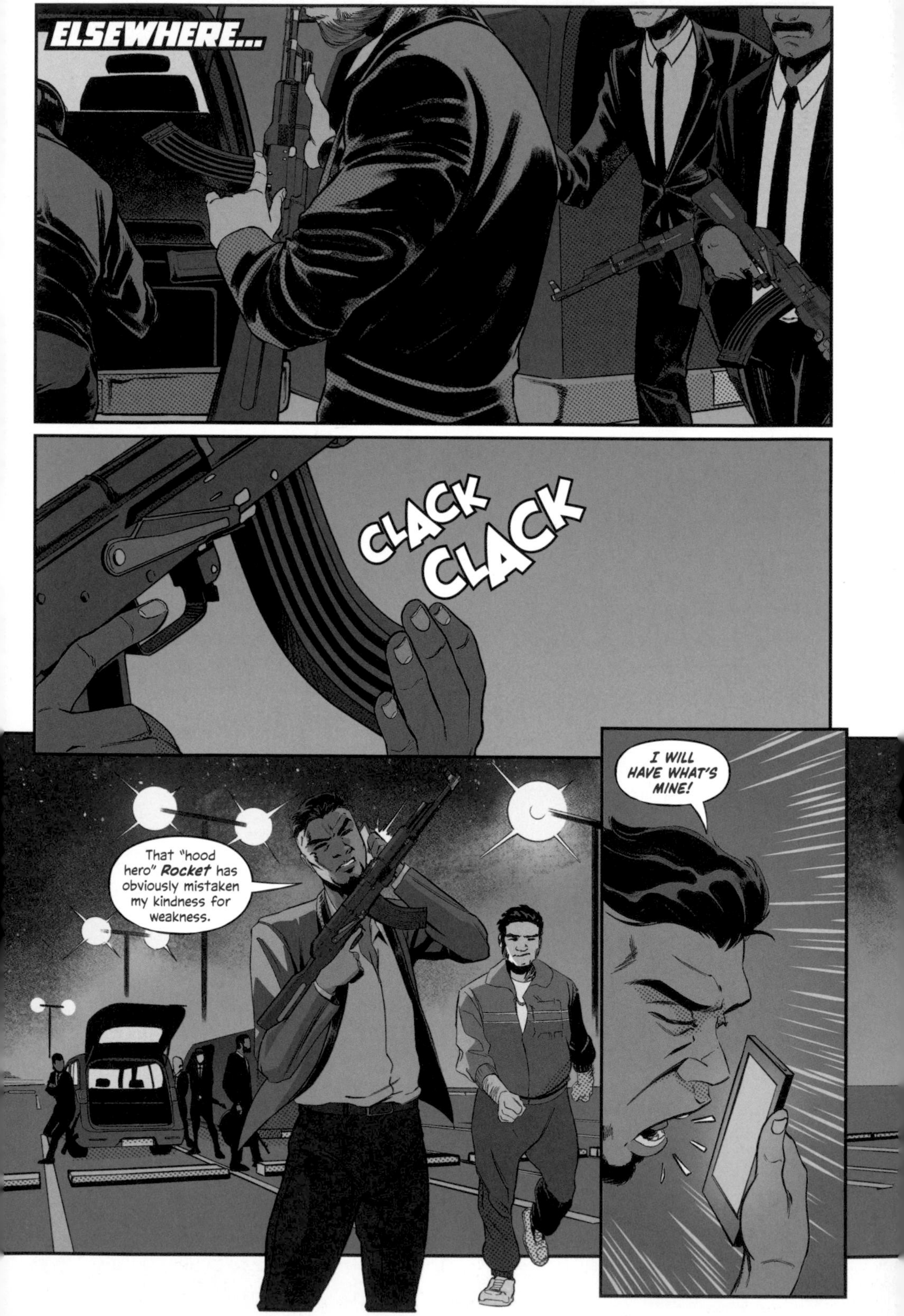
ELSEWHERE...
CLACK
CLACK
That "hood hero" Rocket has obviously mistaken my kindness for weakness.
I WILL HAVE WHAT'S MINE!

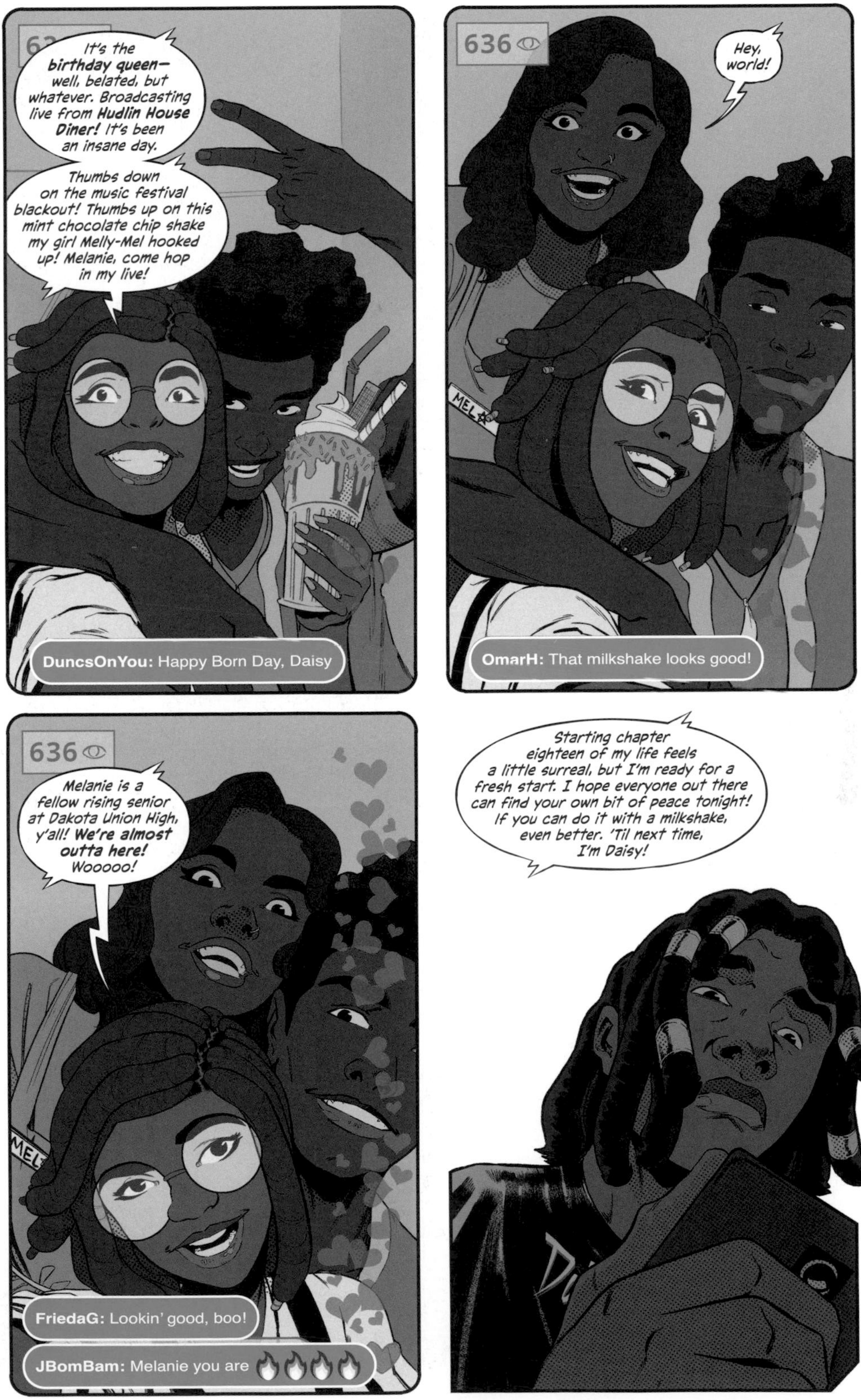
It's the **birthday queen—** well, belated, but whatever. Broadcasting live from **Hudlin House Diner!** It's been an insane day.
Thumbs down on the music festival blackout! Thumbs up on this mint chocolate chip shake my girl Melly-Mel hooked up! Melanie, come hop in my live!
DuncsOnYou: Happy Born Day, Daisy
636
Hey, world!
MEL
OmarH: That milkshake looks good!
636
Melanie is a fellow rising senior at Dakota Union High, y'all! **We're almost outta here!** Wooooo!
FriedaG: Lookin' good, boo!
JBomBam: Melanie you are 🔥🔥🔥🔥
Starting chapter eighteen of my life feels a little surreal, but I'm ready for a fresh start. I hope everyone out there can find your own bit of peace tonight! If you can do it with a milkshake, even better. 'Til next time, I'm Daisy!

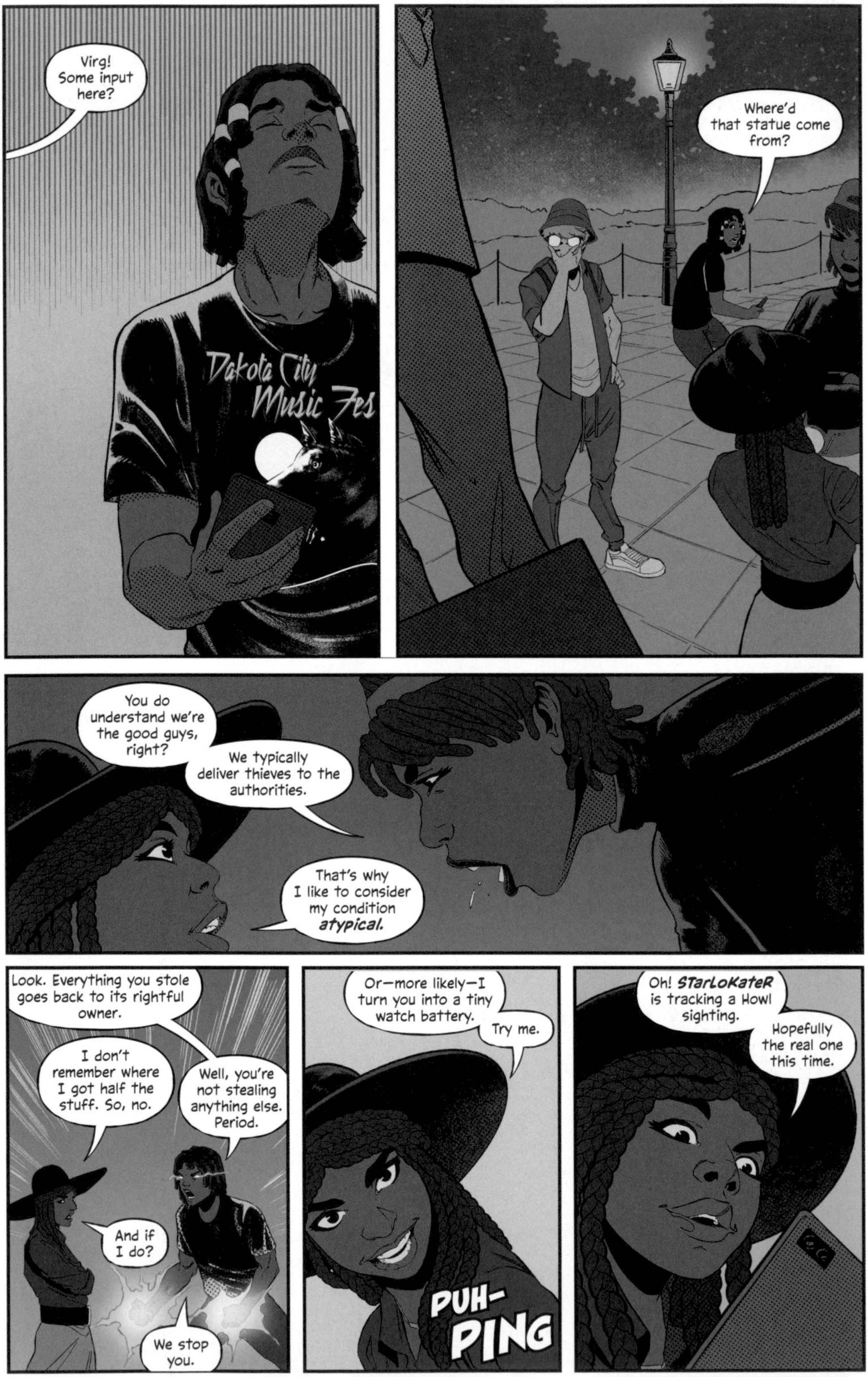
Virg! Some input here?
Where'd that statue come from?
Dakota City Music Fes
You do understand we're the good guys, right?
We typically deliver thieves to the authorities.
That's why I like to consider my condition *atypical.*
Look. Everything you stole goes back to its rightful owner.
I don't remember where I got half the stuff. So, no.
Well, you're not stealing anything else. Period.
And if I do?
We stop you.
Or—more likely—I turn you into a tiny watch battery.
Try me.
PUH-PING
Oh! ***STarLoKateR*** is tracking a Howl sighting.
Hopefully the real one this time.

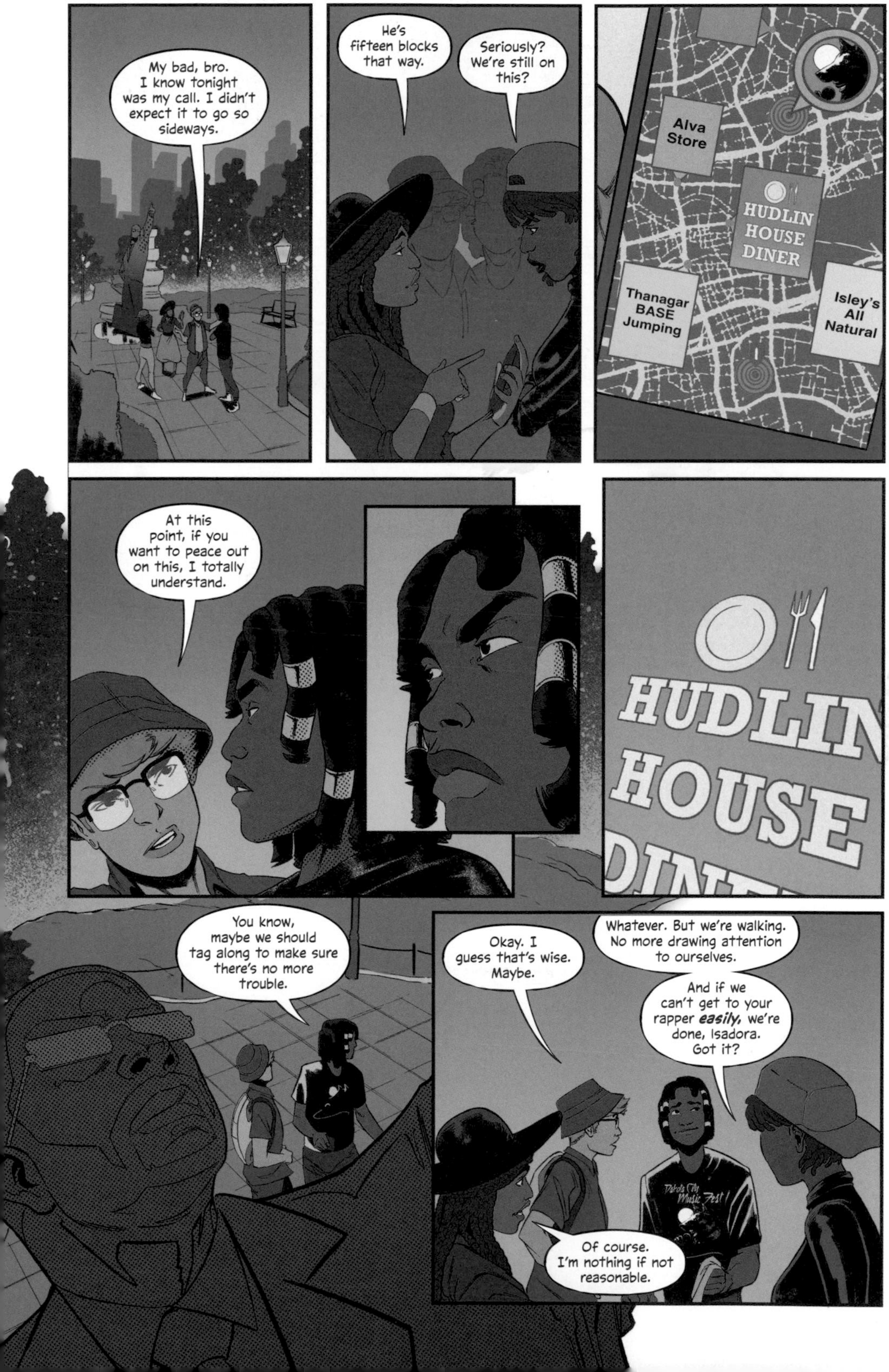

My bad, bro. I know tonight was my call. I didn't expect it to go so sideways.
He's fifteen blocks that way.
Seriously? We're still on this?
Alva Store
HUDLIN HOUSE DINER
Thanagar BASE Jumping
Isley's All Natural
At this point, if you want to peace out on this, I totally understand.
HUDLIN HOUSE
You know, maybe we should tag along to make sure there's no more trouble.
Okay. I guess that's wise. Maybe.
Whatever. But we're walking. No more drawing attention to ourselves.
And if we can't get to your rapper ***easily,*** we're done, Isadora. Got it?
Of course. I'm nothing if not reasonable.

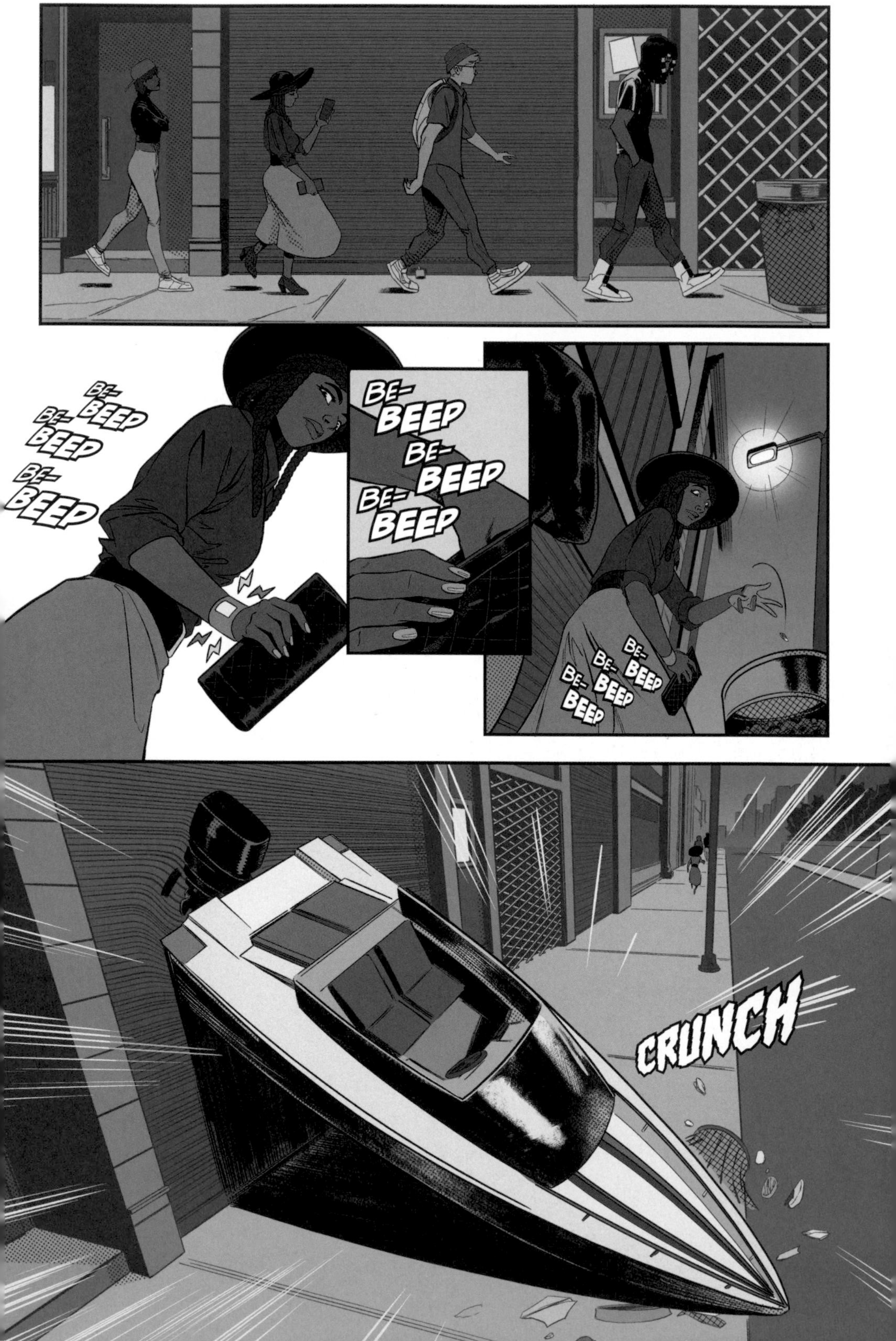

BE-BEEP
BE-BEEP
BE-BEEP
BE-BEEP
BE-BEEP
BE-BEEP
BE-BEEP
BE-BEEP
BE-BEEP
CRUNCH

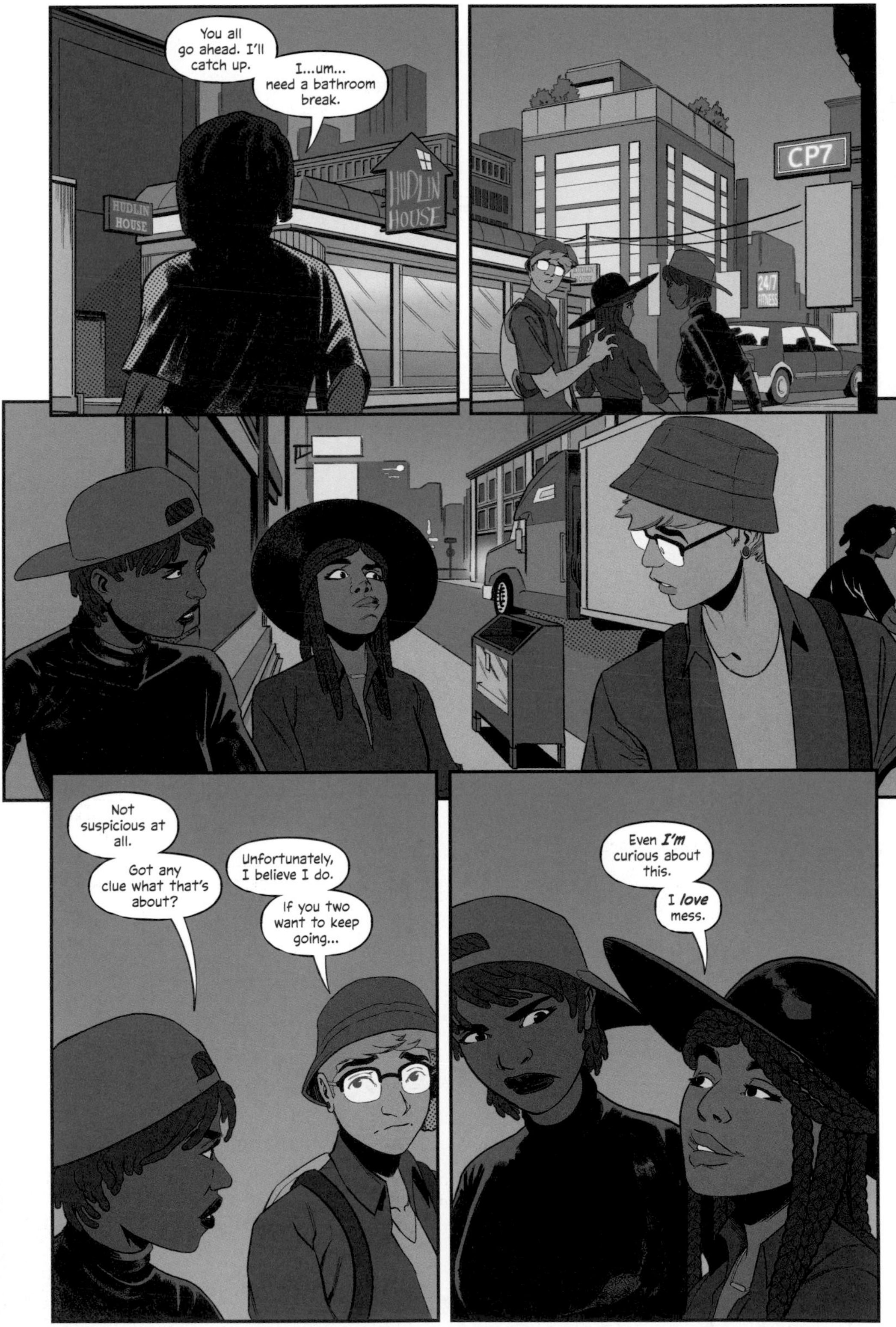

You all go ahead. I'll catch up.
I...um... need a bathroom break.
HUDLIN HOUSE
HUDLIN HOUSE
CP7
24/7 FITNESS
Not suspicious at all.
Got any clue what that's about?
Unfortunately, I believe I do.
If you two want to keep going...
Even *I'm* curious about this.
I *love* mess.

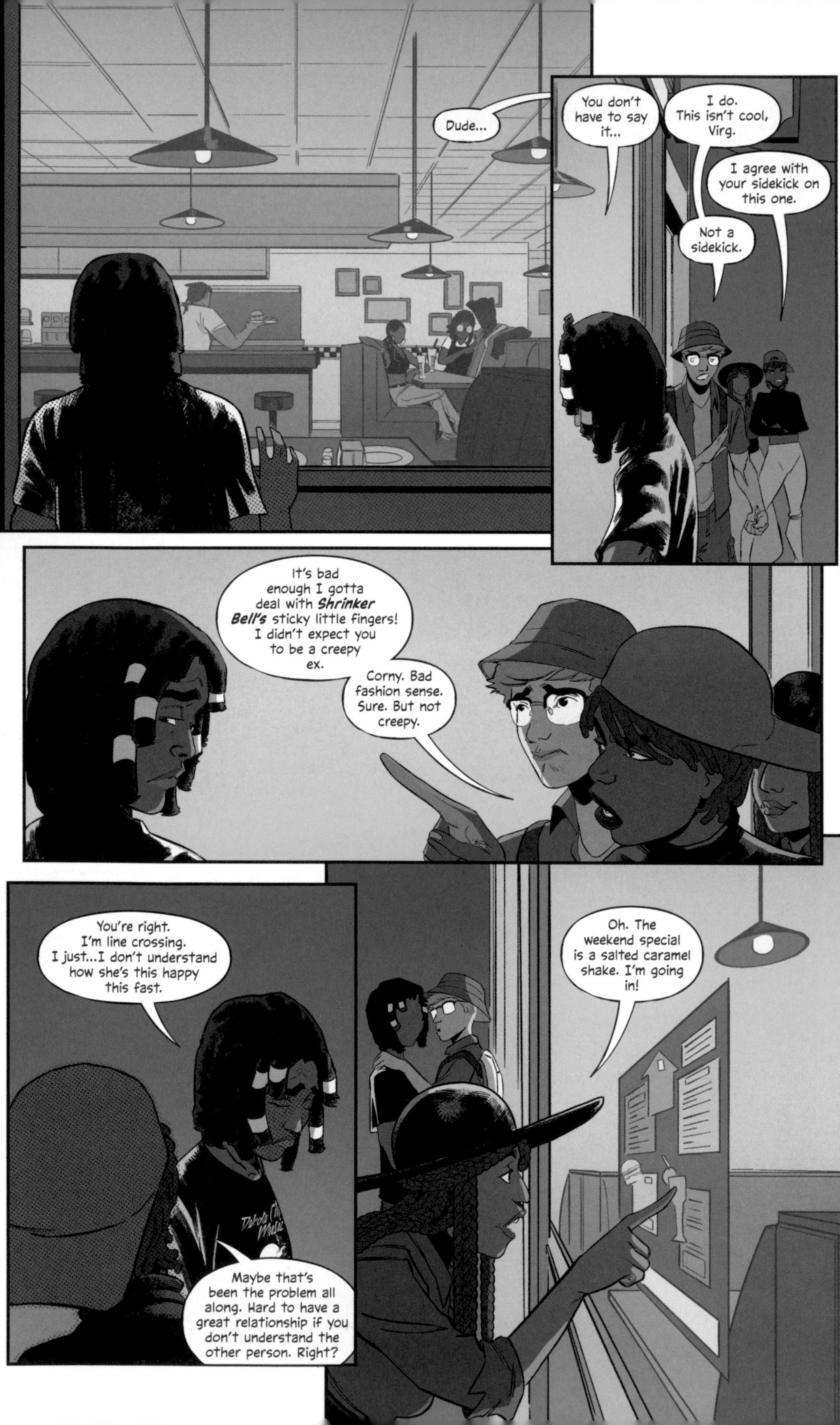
Dude...
You don't have to say it...
I do. This isn't cool, Virg.
I agree with your sidekick on this one.
Not a sidekick.
It's bad enough I gotta deal with **Shrinker Bell's** sticky little fingers! I didn't expect you to be a creepy ex.
Corny. Bad fashion sense. Sure. But not creepy.
You're right. I'm line crossing. I just...I don't understand how she's this happy this fast.
Oh. The weekend special is a salted caramel shake. I'm going in!
Maybe that's been the problem all along. Hard to have a great relationship if you don't understand the other person. Right?

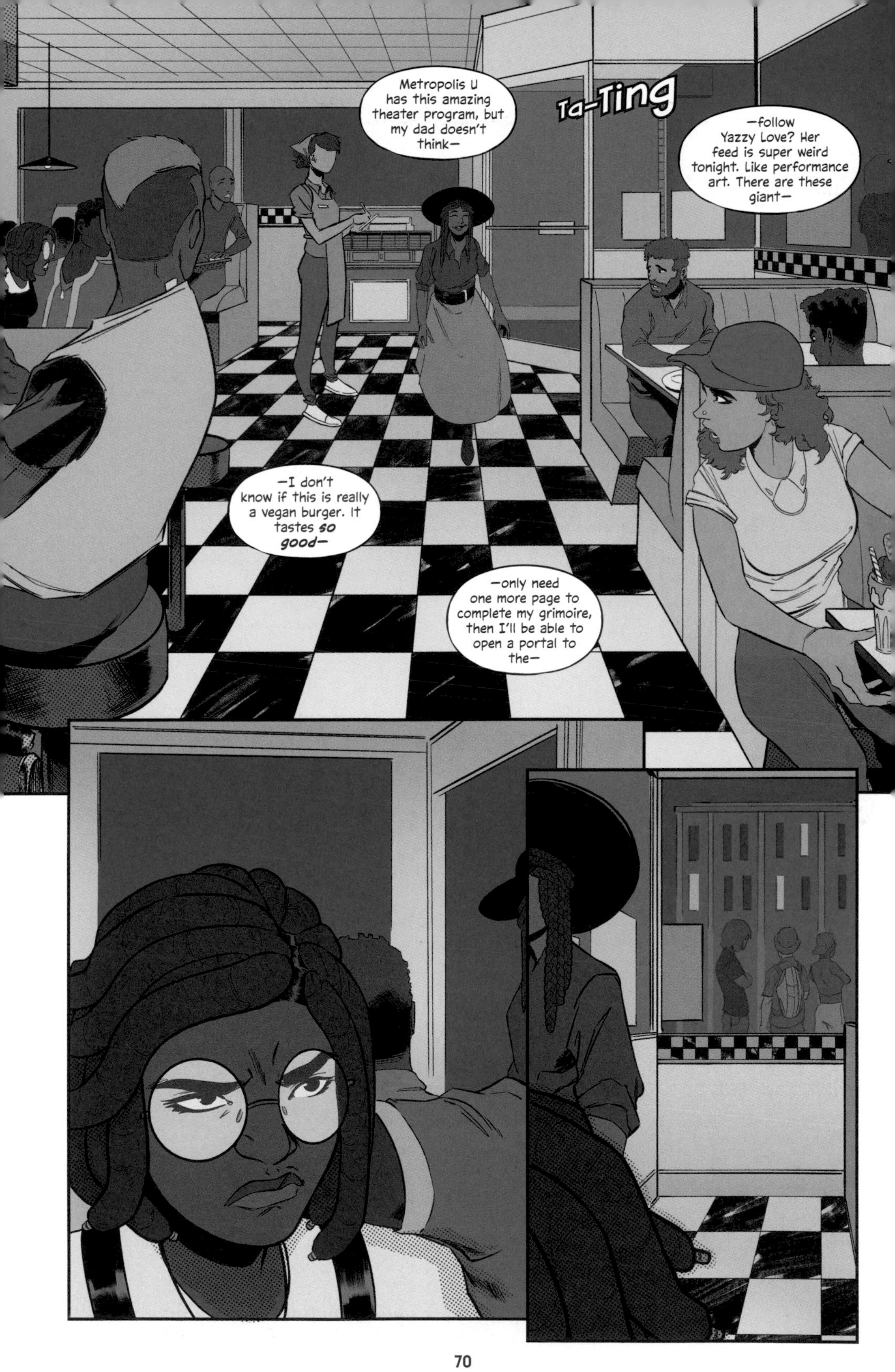
Metropolis U has this amazing theater program, but my dad doesn't think—
Ta-Ting
—follow Yazzy Love? Her feed is super weird tonight. Like performance art. There are these giant—
—I don't know if this is really a vegan burger. It tastes so good—
—only need one more page to complete my grimoire, then I'll be able to open a portal to the—

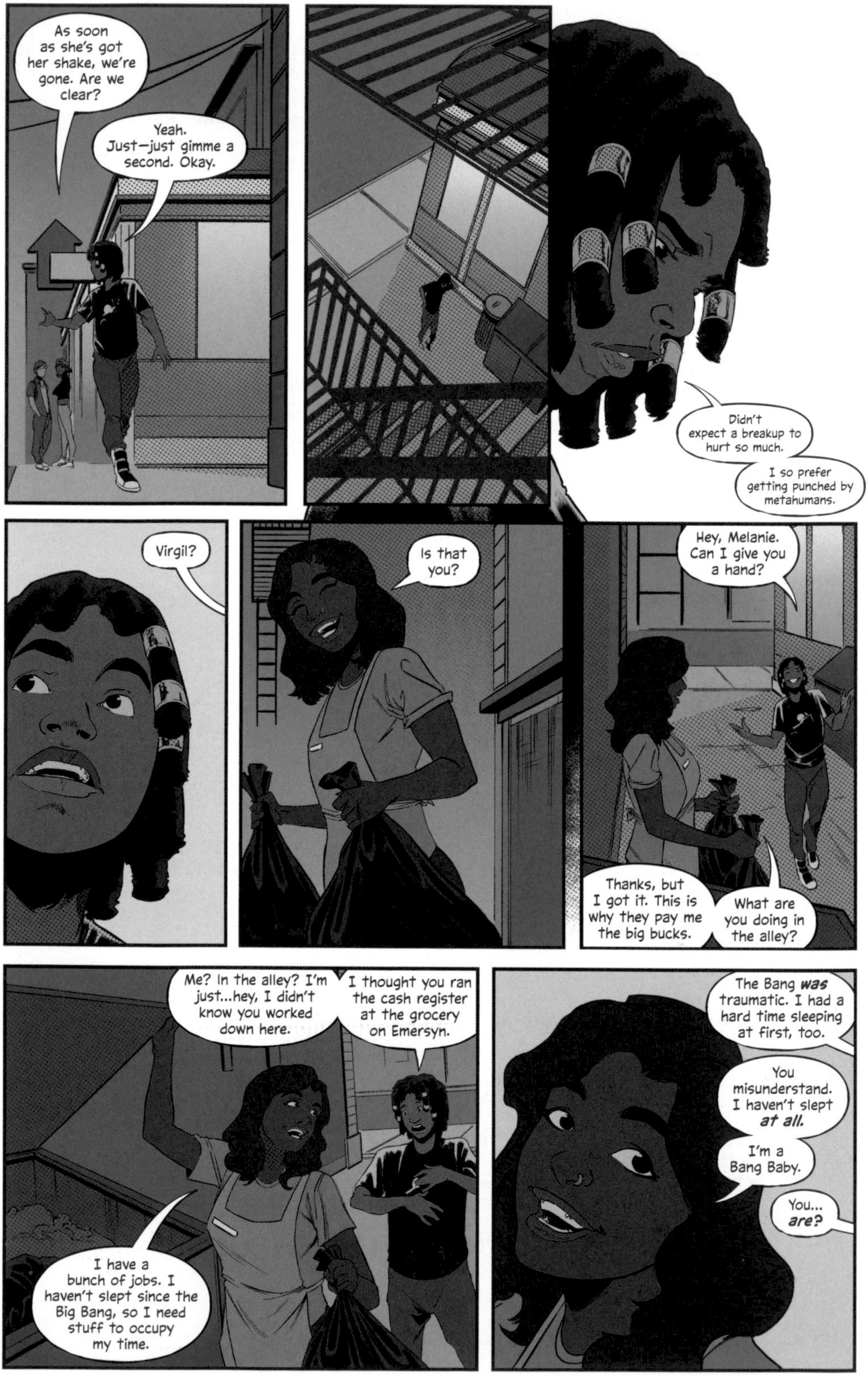
As soon as she's got her shake, we're gone. Are we clear?
Yeah. Just—just gimme a second. Okay.
Didn't expect a breakup to hurt so much.
I so prefer getting punched by metahumans.
Virgil?
Is that you?
Hey, Melanie. Can I give you a hand?
Thanks, but I got it. This is why they pay me the big bucks.
What are you doing in the alley?
Me? In the alley? I'm just...hey, I didn't know you worked down here.
I thought you ran the cash register at the grocery on Emersyn.
I have a bunch of jobs. I haven't slept since the Big Bang, so I need stuff to occupy my time.
The Bang *was* traumatic. I had a hard time sleeping at first, too.
You misunderstand. I haven't slept *at all.*
I'm a Bang Baby.
You... *are?*

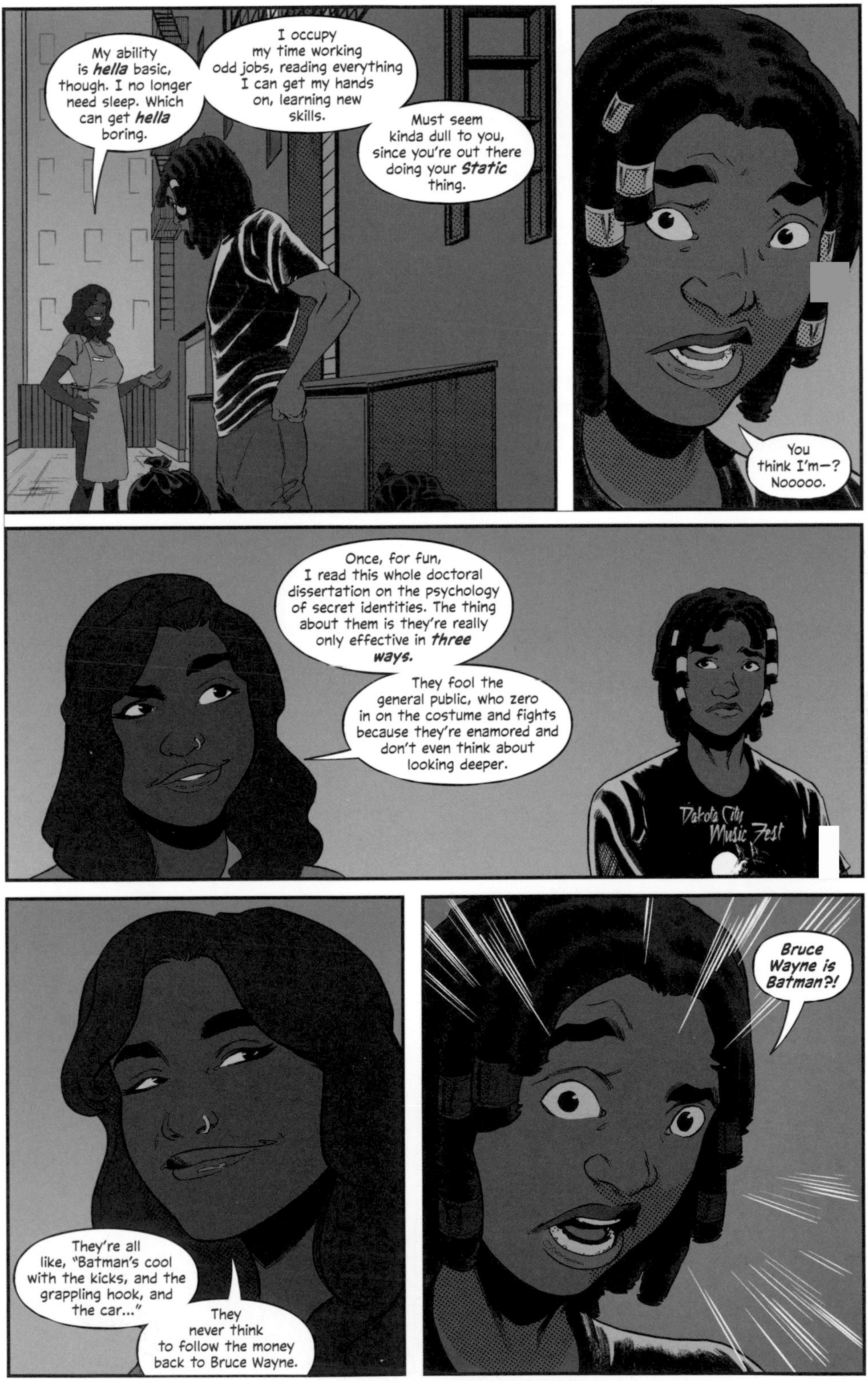
My ability is *hella* basic, though. I no longer need sleep. Which can get *hella* boring.
I occupy my time working odd jobs, reading everything I can get my hands on, learning new skills.
Must seem kinda dull to you, since you're out there doing your *Static* thing.
You think I'm—? Nooooo.
Once, for fun, I read this whole doctoral dissertation on the psychology of secret identities. The thing about them is they're really only effective in *three ways.*
They fool the general public, who zero in on the costume and fights because they're enamored and don't even think about looking deeper.
Dakota City Music Fest
They're all like, "Batman's cool with the kicks, and the grappling hook, and the car..."
They never think to follow the money back to Bruce Wayne.
Bruce Wayne is Batman?!

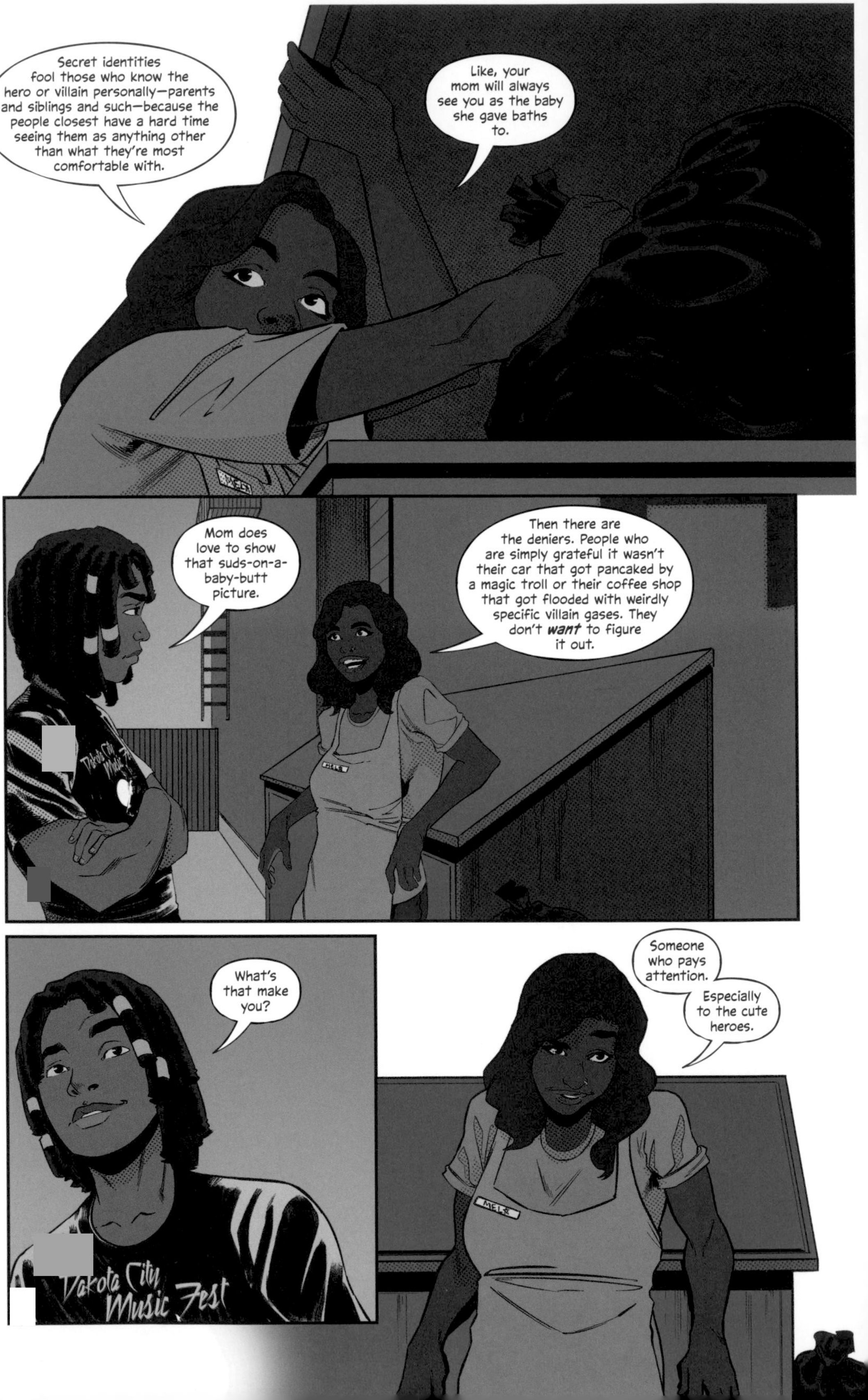
Secret identities fool those who know the hero or villain personally—parents and siblings and such—because the people closest have a hard time seeing them as anything other than what they're most comfortable with.
Like, your mom will always see you as the baby she gave baths to.
Mom does love to show that suds-on-a-baby-butt picture.
Then there are the deniers. People who are simply grateful it wasn't their car that got pancaked by a magic troll or their coffee shop that got flooded with weirdly specific villain gases. They don't ***want*** to figure it out.
What's that make you?
Someone who pays attention.
Especially to the cute heroes.
Dakota City Music Fest
MEL

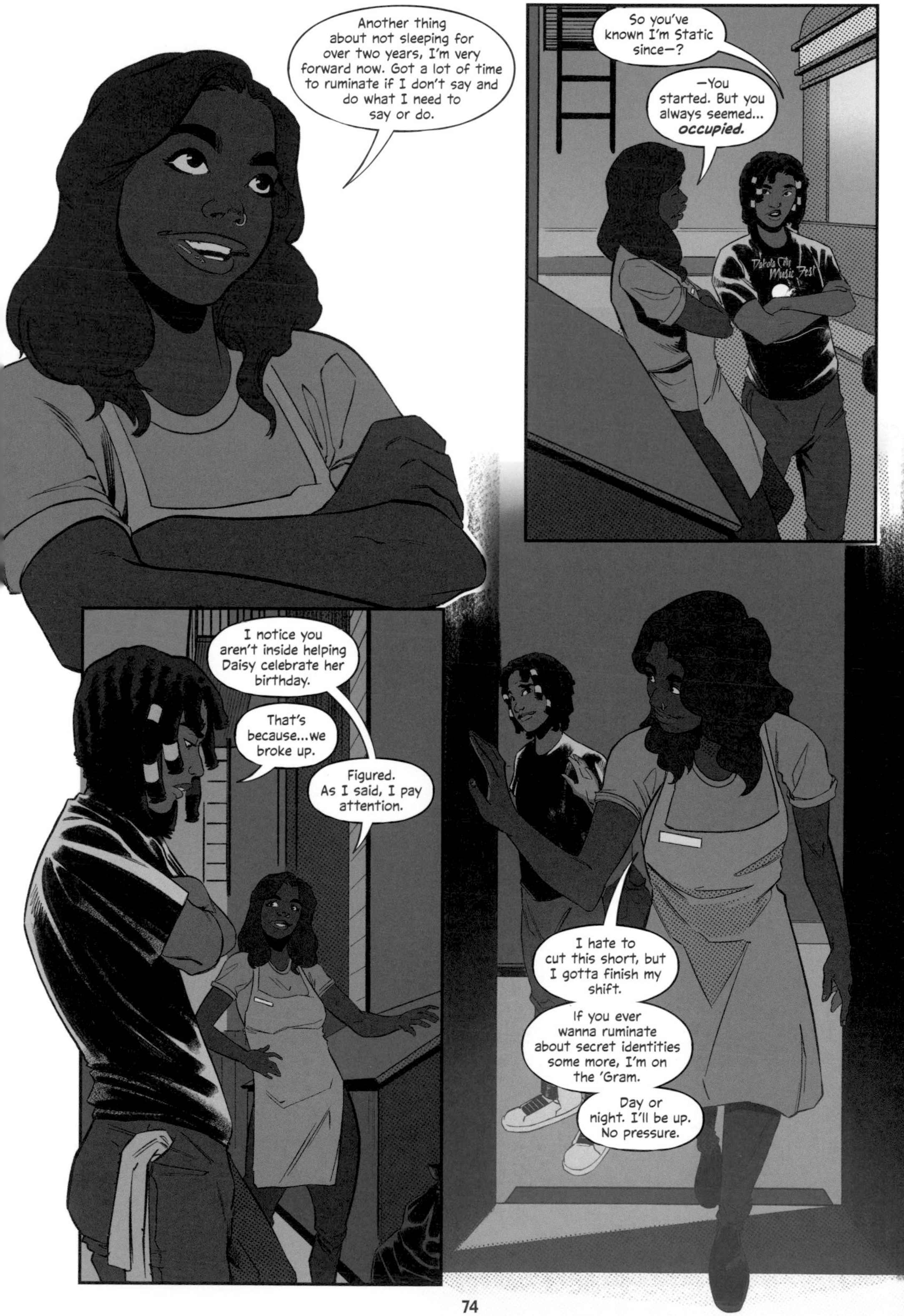
Another thing about not sleeping for over two years, I'm very forward now. Got a lot of time to ruminate if I don't say and do what I need to say or do.
So you've known I'm Static since—?
—You started. But you always seemed... *occupied.*
Dakota City Music Fest
I notice you aren't inside helping Daisy celebrate her birthday.
That's because...we broke up.
Figured. As I said, I pay attention.
I hate to cut this short, but I gotta finish my shift.
If you ever wanna ruminate about secret identities some more, I'm on the 'Gram.
Day or night. I'll be up. No pressure.

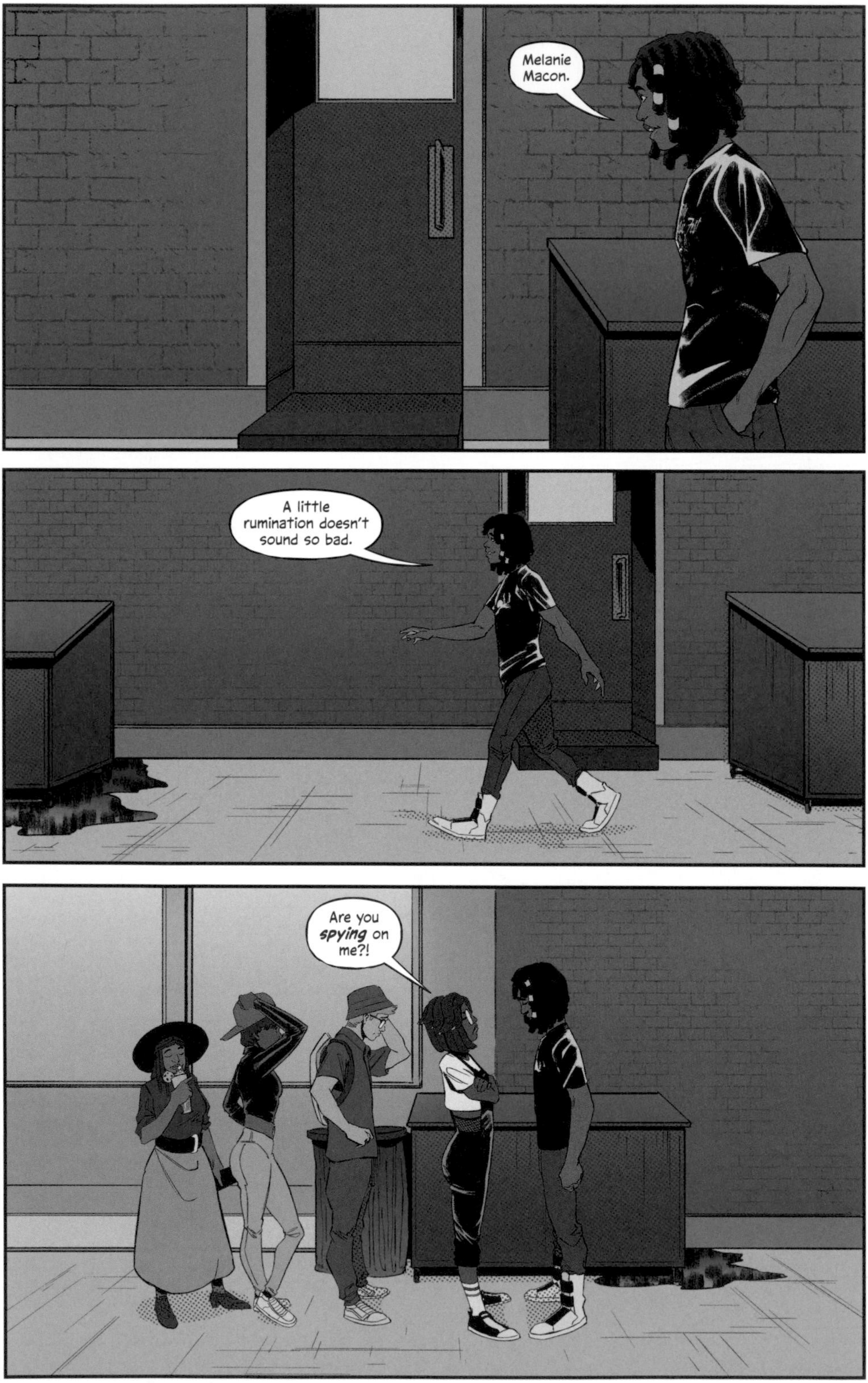
Melanie Macon.
A little rumination doesn't sound so bad.
Are you *spying* on me?!

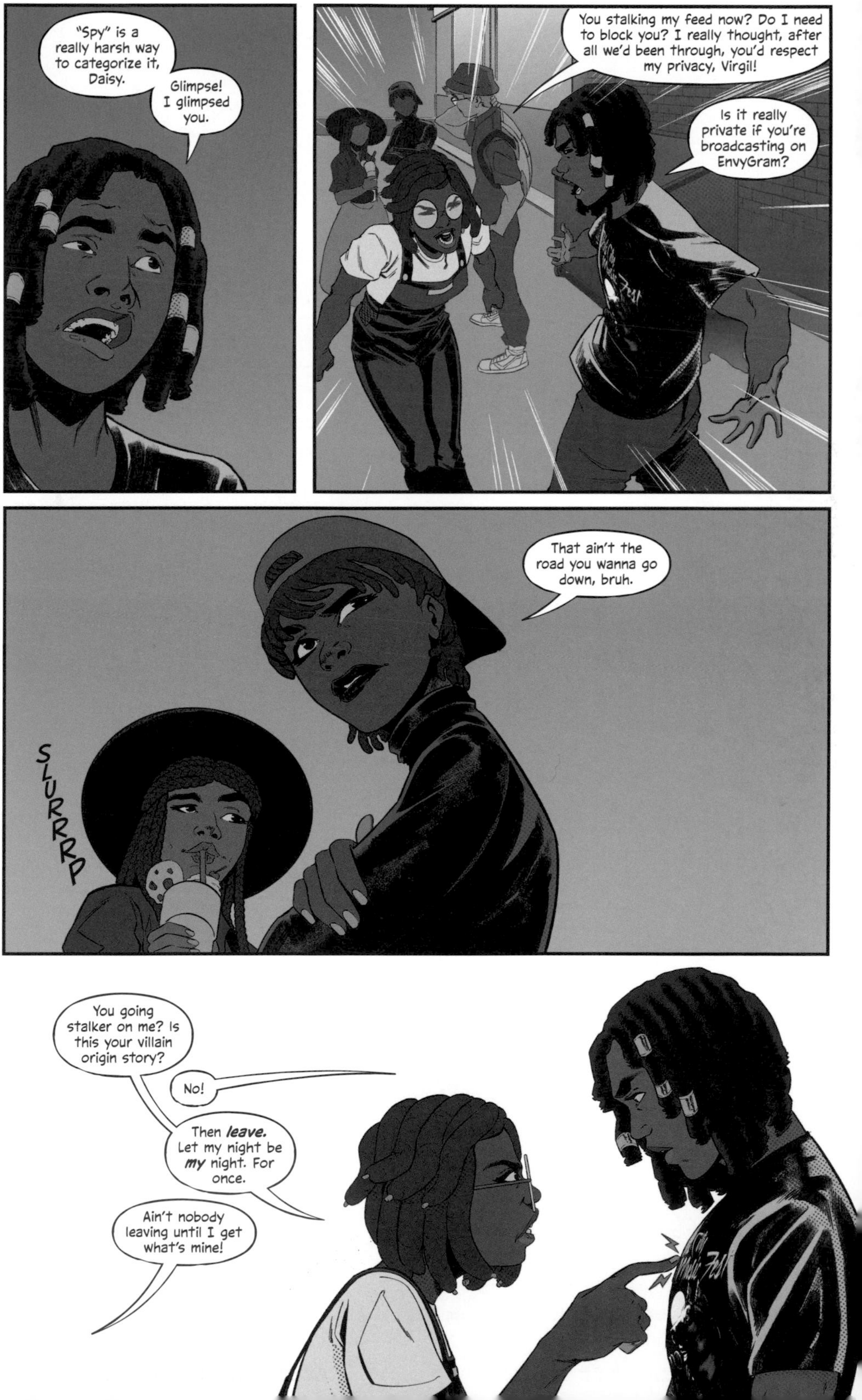
"Spy" is a really harsh way to categorize it, Daisy.
Glimpse! I glimpsed you.
You stalking my feed now? Do I need to block you? I really thought, after all we'd been through, you'd respect my privacy, Virgil!
Is it really private if you're broadcasting on EnvyGram?
That ain't the road you wanna go down, bruh.
SLURRRP
You going stalker on me? Is this your villain origin story?
No!
Then *leave.* Let my night be *my* night. For once.
Ain't nobody leaving until I get what's mine!

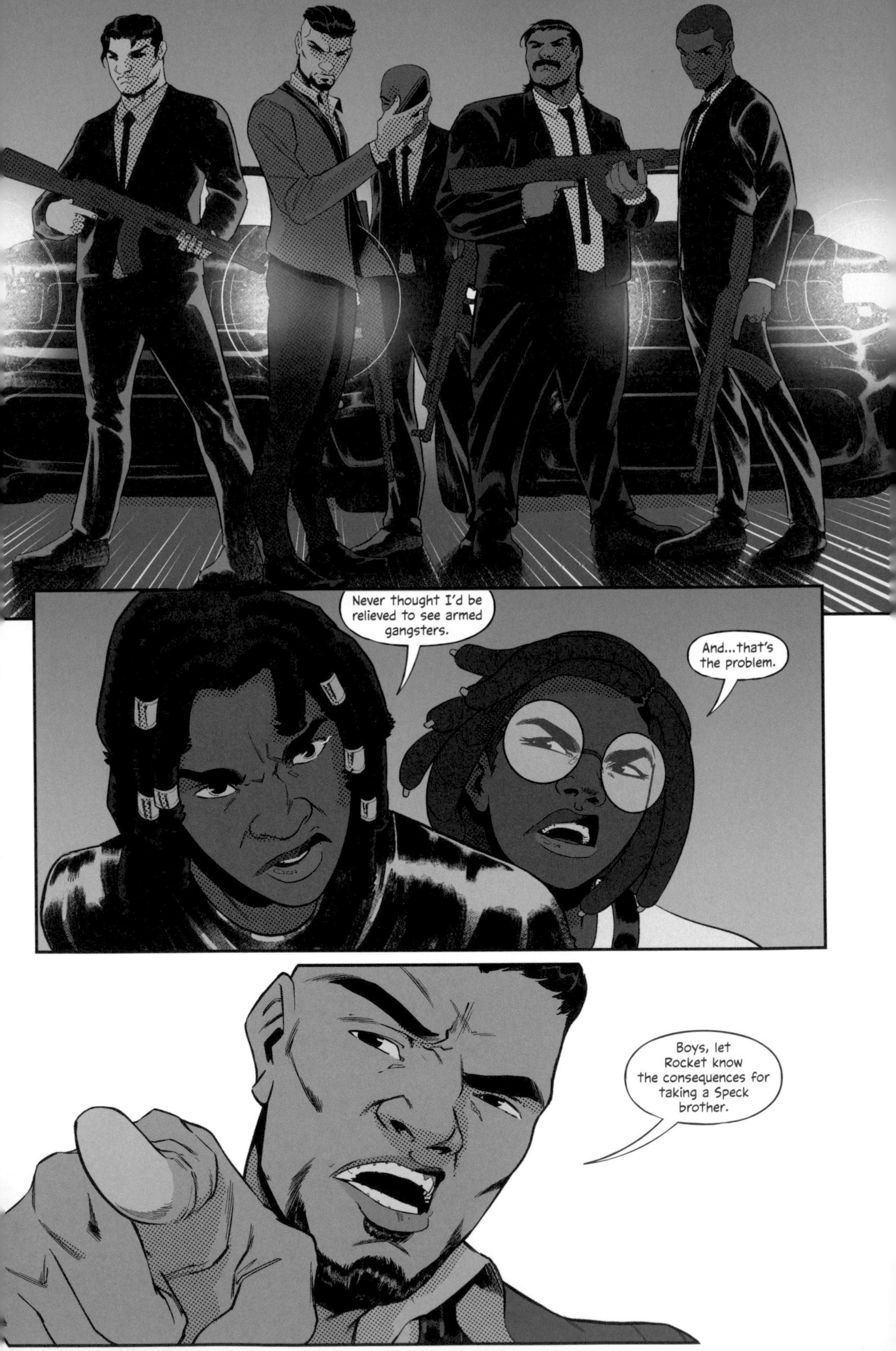
Never thought I'd be relieved to see armed gangsters.
And...that's the problem.
Boys, let Rocket know the consequences for taking a Speck brother.

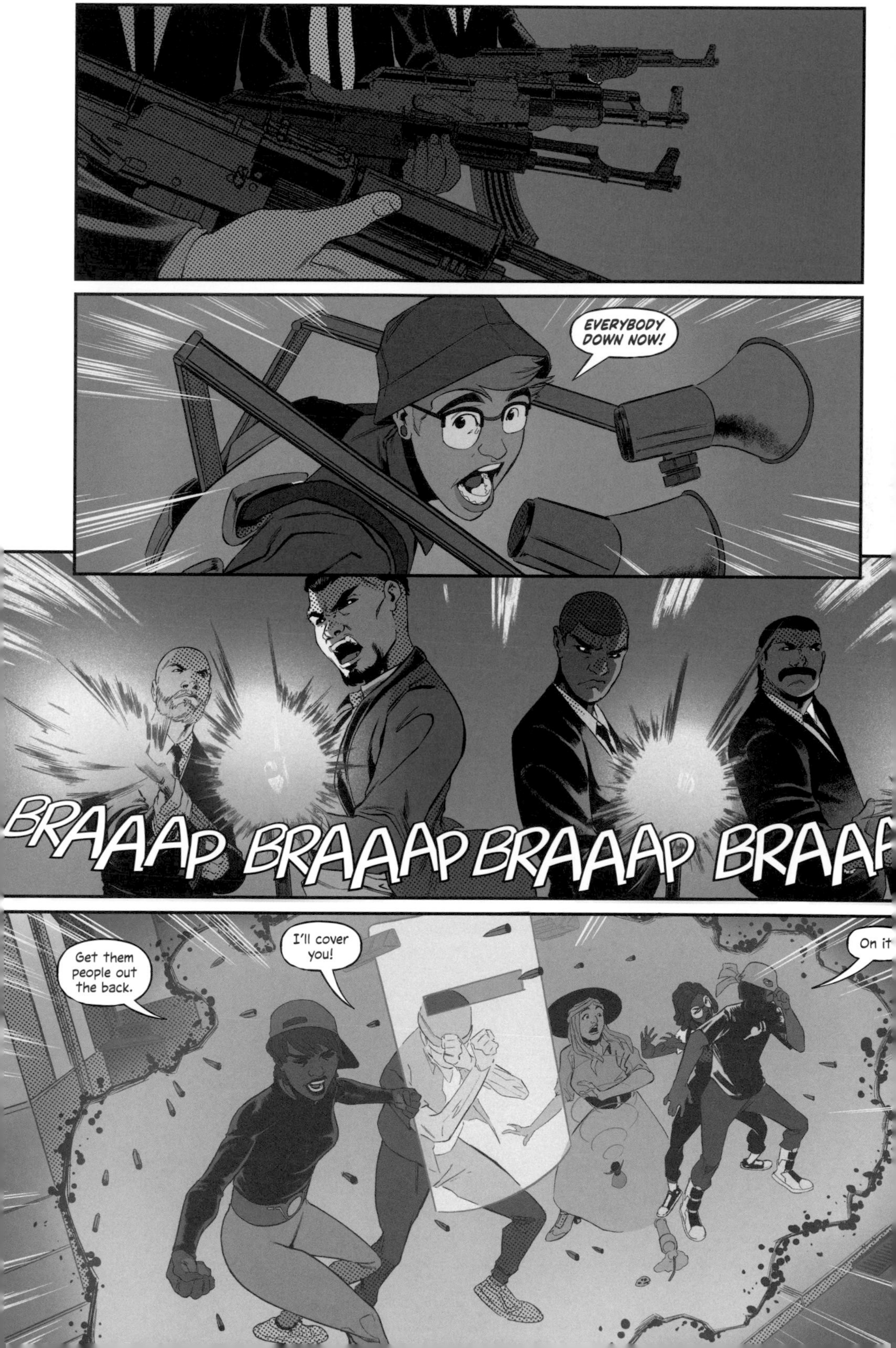
EVERYBODY DOWN NOW!
BRAAAP BRAAAP BRAAAP BRAA
Get them people out the back.
I'll cover you!
On it

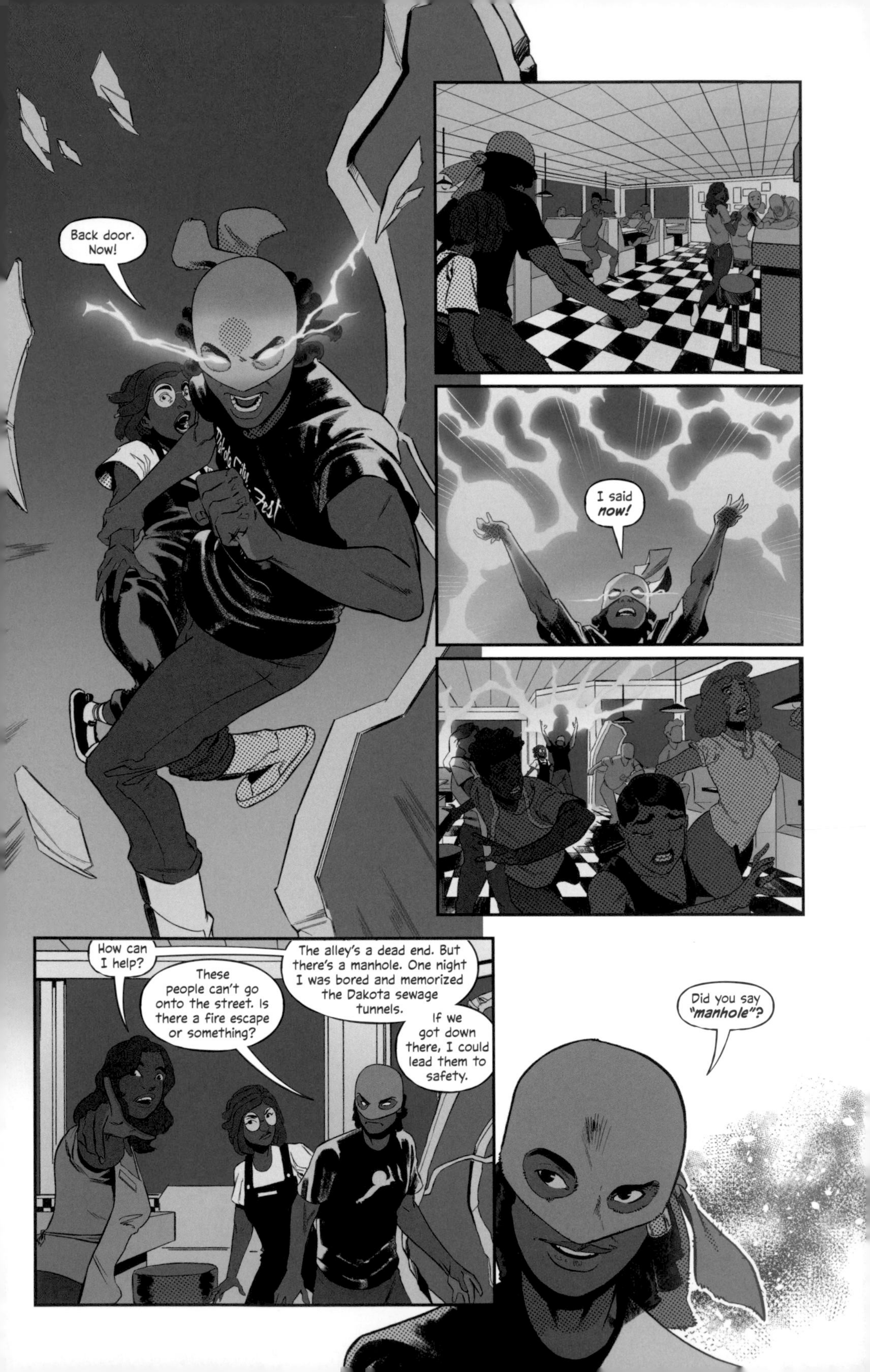
Back door. Now!
Dakota City Fest
I said *now!*
How can I help?
These people can't go onto the street. Is there a fire escape or something?
The alley's a dead end. But there's a manhole. One night I was bored and memorized the Dakota sewage tunnels.
If we got down there, I could lead them to safety.
Did you say ***"manhole"***?

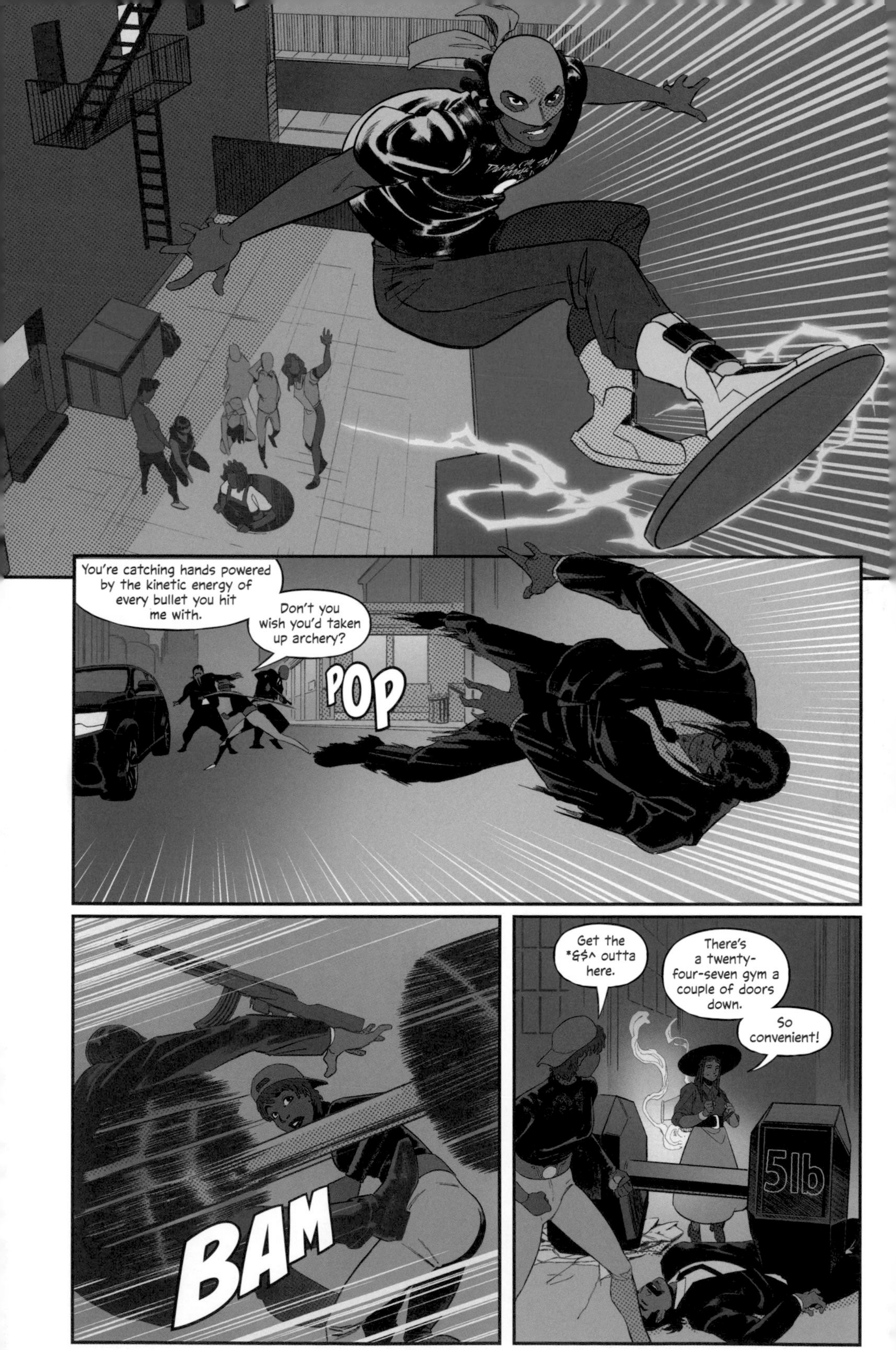
You're catching hands powered by the kinetic energy of every bullet you hit me with.
Don't you wish you'd taken up archery?
POP
BAM
Get the *&$^ outta here.
There's a twenty-four-seven gym a couple of doors down.
So convenient!
5lb

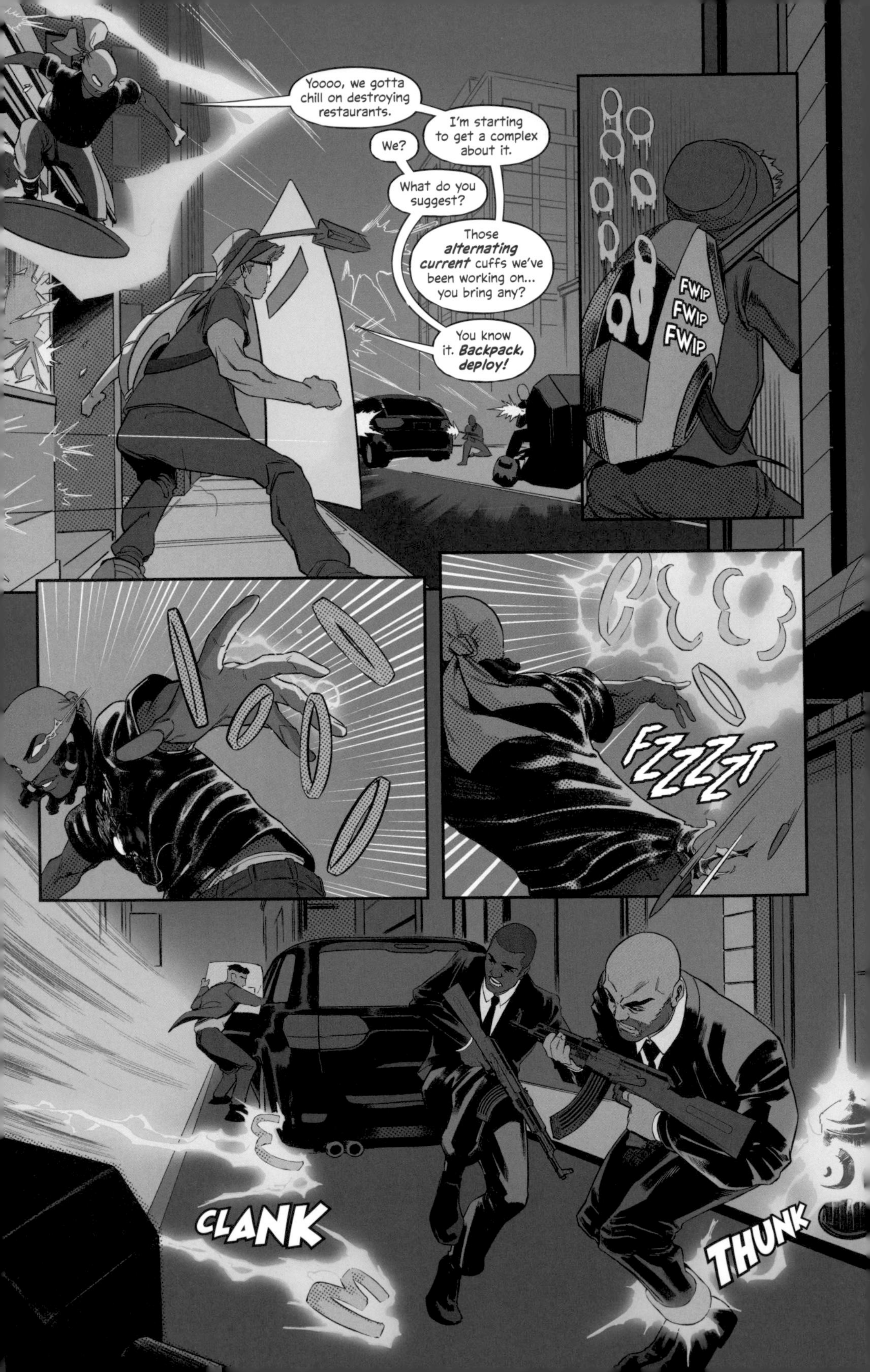

Yoooo, we gotta chill on destroying restaurants.
I'm starting to get a complex about it.
We?
What do you suggest?
Those ***alternating current*** cuffs we've been working on... you bring any?
You know it. ***Backpack, deploy!***
FWIP FWIP FWIP
FZZZZZT
CLANK
THUNK

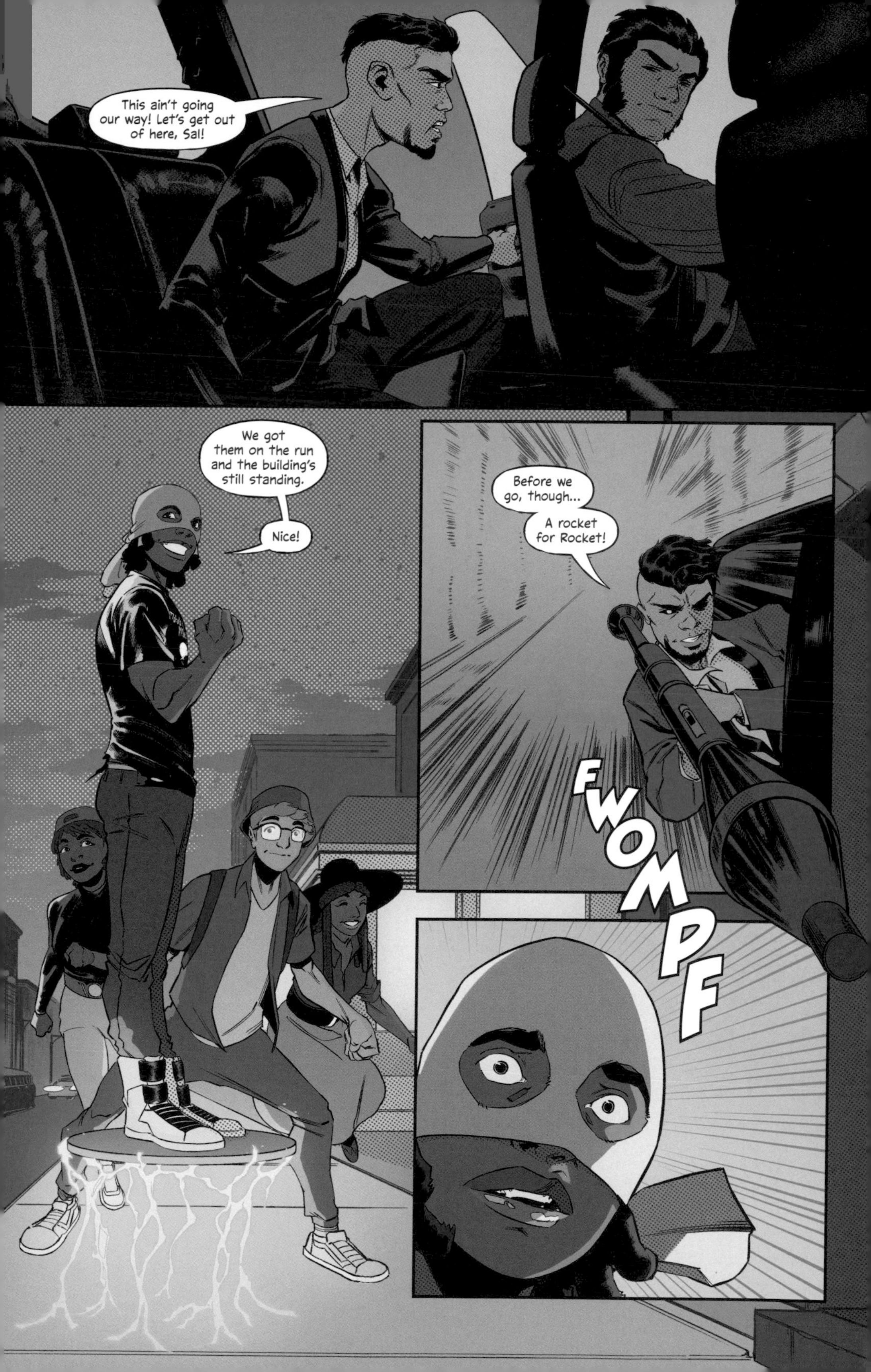
This ain't going our way! Let's get out of here, Sal!
We got them on the run and the building's still standing.
Nice!
Before we go, though...
A rocket for Rocket!
FWOMPF

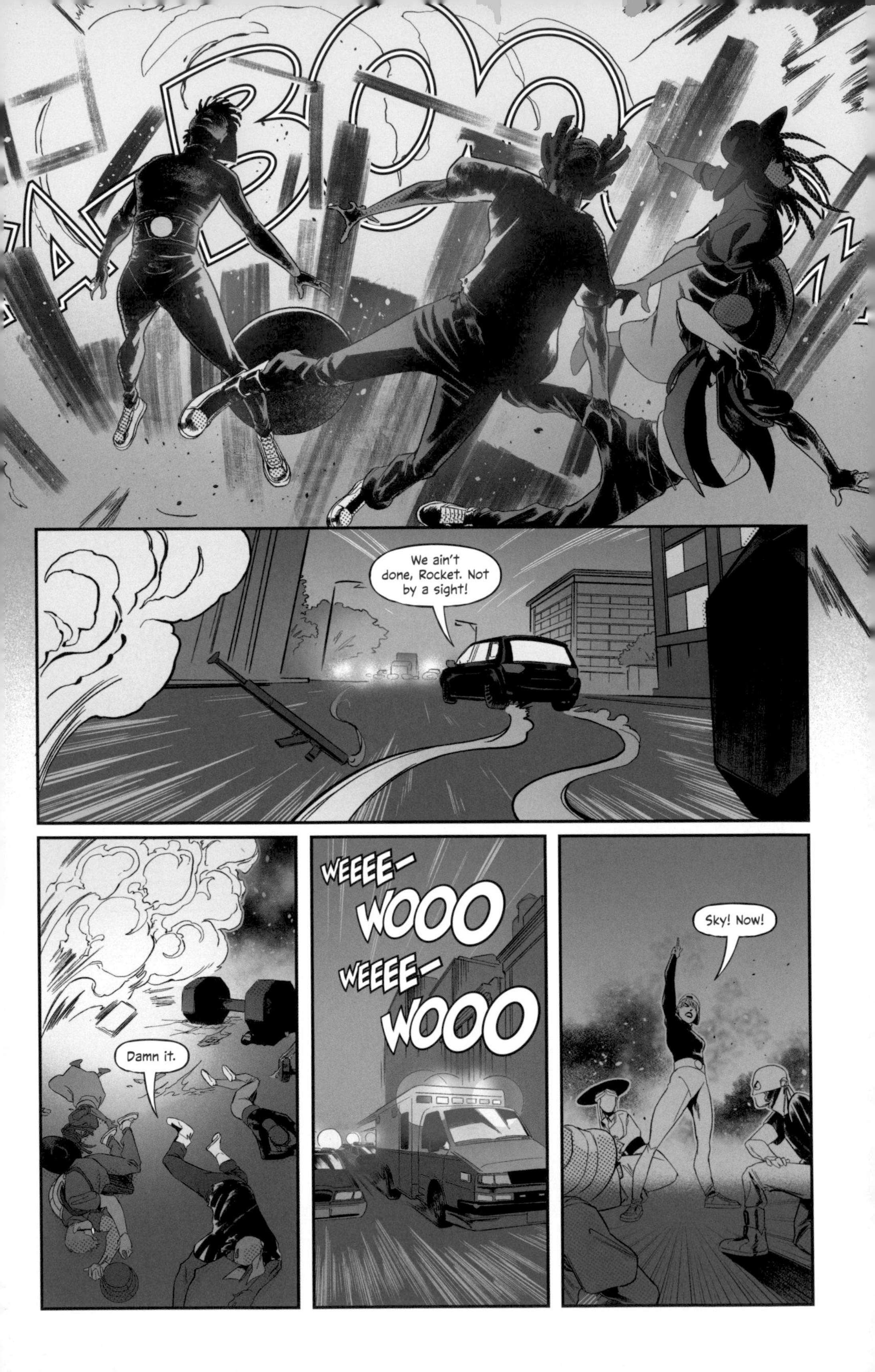
We ain't done, Rocket. Not by a sight!
Damn it.
WEEEE-
WOOO
WEEEE-
WOOO
Sky! Now!

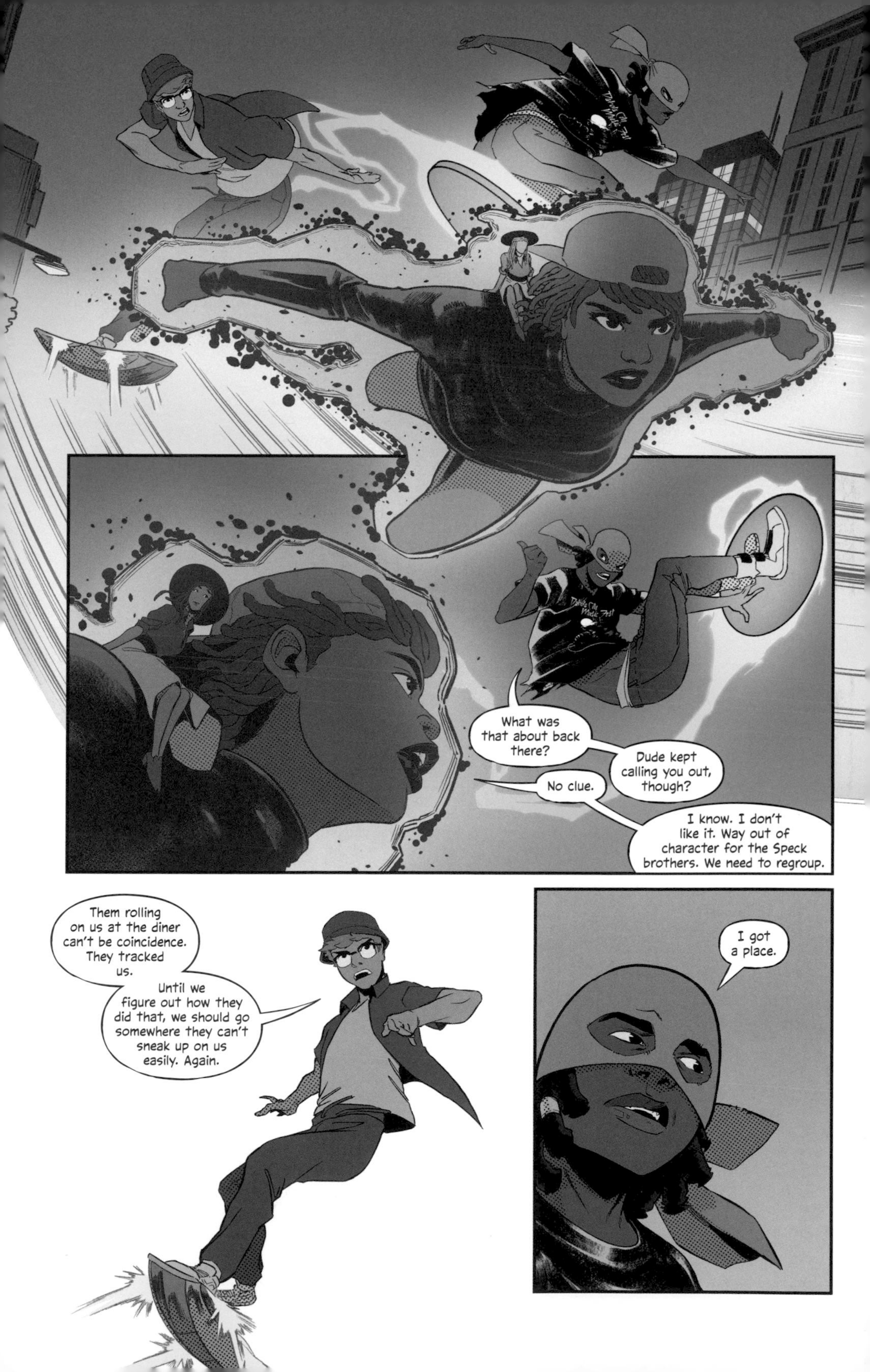
What was that about back there?
Dude kept calling you out, though?
No clue.
I know. I don't like it. Way out of character for the Speck brothers. We need to regroup.
Them rolling on us at the diner can't be coincidence. They tracked us.
Until we figure out how they did that, we should go somewhere they can't sneak up on us easily. Again.
I got a place.

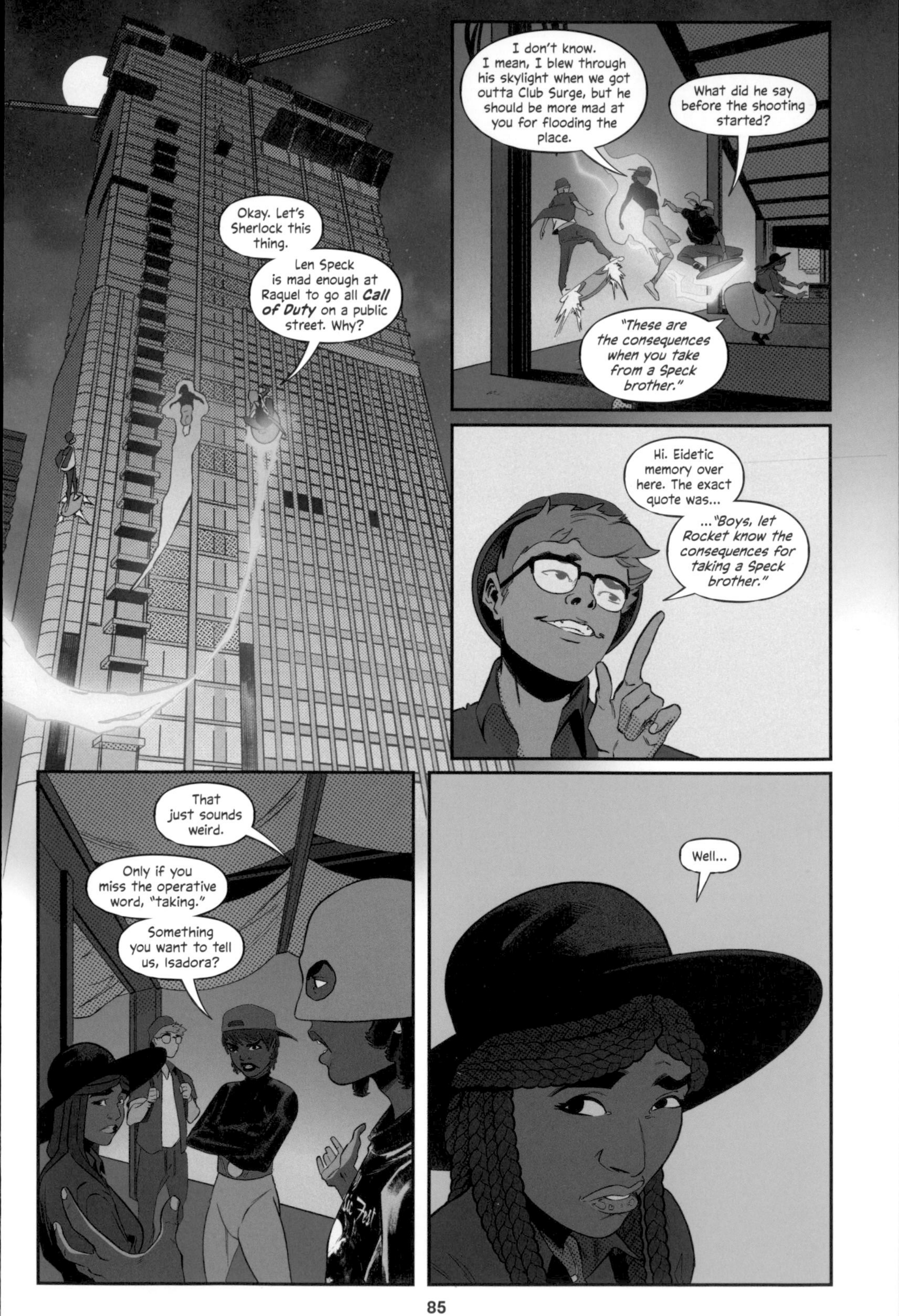
Okay. Let's Sherlock this thing.
Len Speck is mad enough at Raquel to go all **Call of Duty** on a public street. Why?
I don't know. I mean, I blew through his skylight when we got outta Club Surge, but he should be more mad at you for flooding the place.
What did he say before the shooting started?
"These are the consequences when you take from a Speck brother."
Hi. Eidetic memory over here. The exact quote was...
..."Boys, let Rocket know the consequences for taking a Speck brother."
That just sounds weird.
Only if you miss the operative word, "taking."
Something you want to tell us, Isadora?
Well...

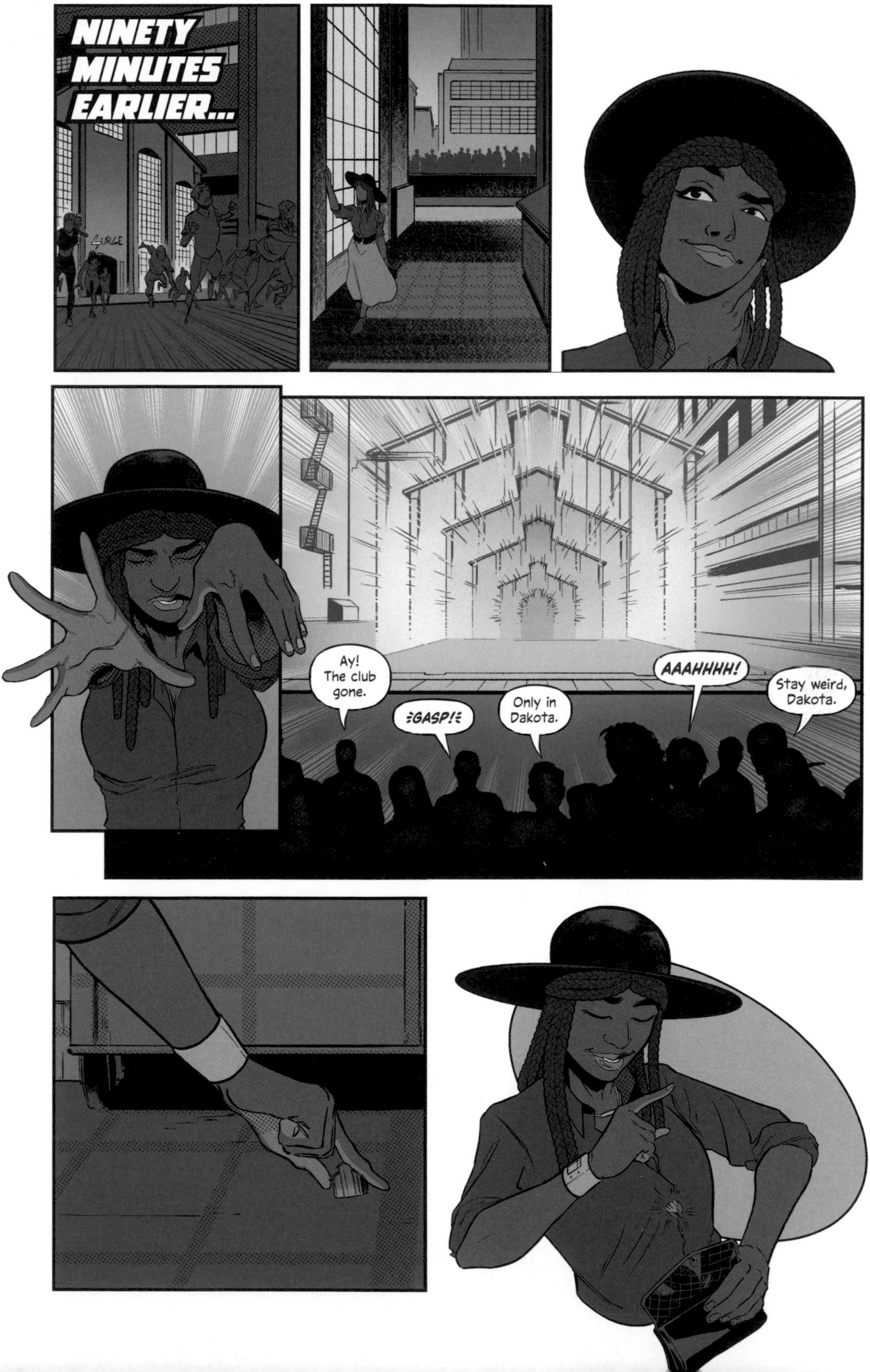
NINETY MINUTES EARLIER...
SURGE
Ay! The club gone.
GASP!
Only in Dakota.
AAAHHHH!
Stay weird, Dakota.

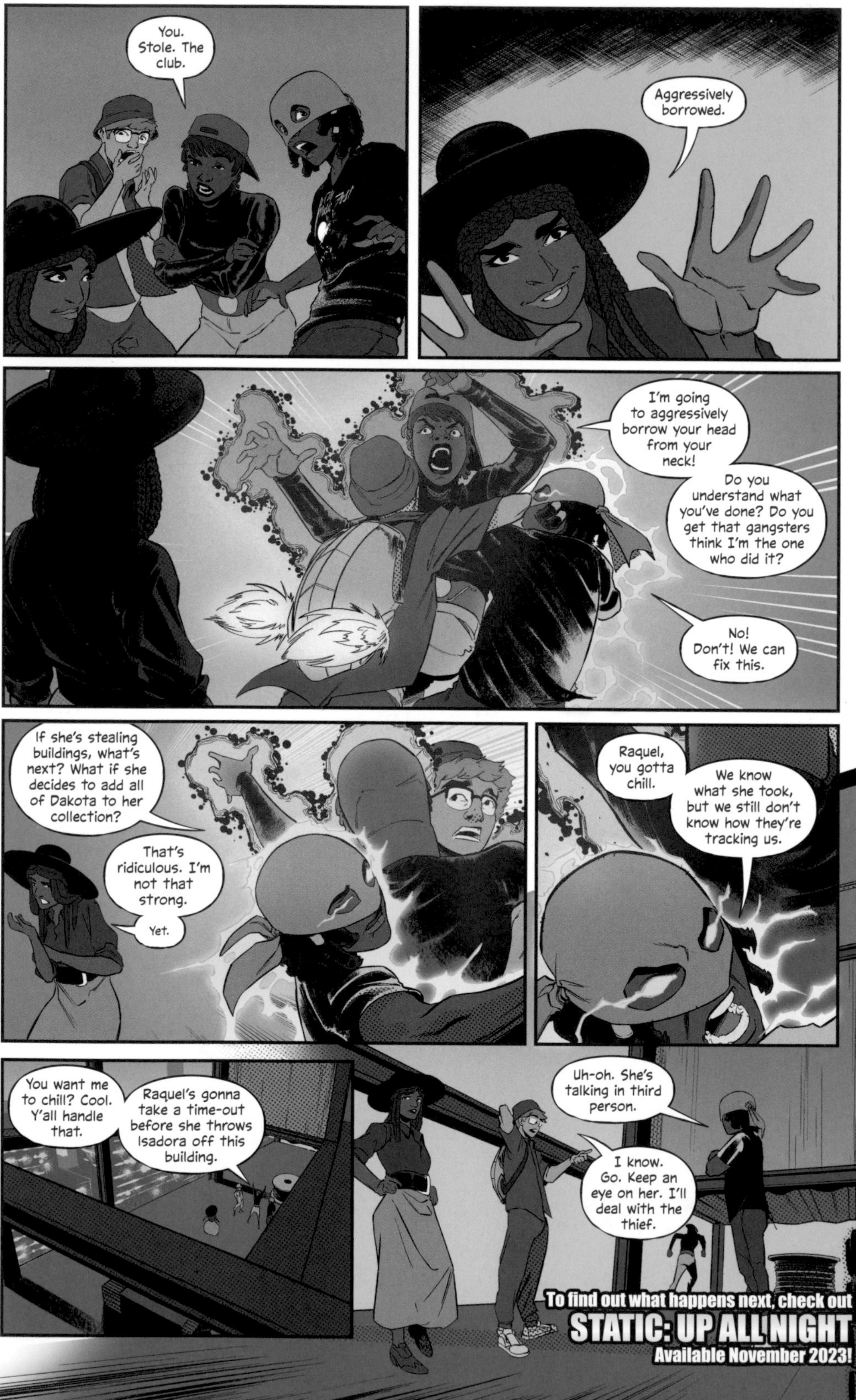
You. Stole. The club.
Aggressively borrowed.
I'm going to aggressively borrow your head from your neck!
Do you understand what you've done? Do you get that gangsters think I'm the one who did it?
No! Don't! We can fix this.
If she's stealing buildings, what's next? What if she decides to add all of Dakota to her collection?
That's ridiculous. I'm not that strong.
Yet.
Raquel, you gotta chill.
We know what she took, but we still don't know how they're tracking us.
You want me to chill? Cool. Y'all handle that.
Raquel's gonna take a time-out before she throws Isadora off this building.
Uh-oh. She's talking in third person.
I know. Go. Keep an eye on her. I'll deal with the thief.
To find out what happens next, check out
STATIC: UP ALL NIGHT
Available November 2023!

Lamar Giles writes for teens and adults across multiple genres, with work appearing on numerous Best Of lists each and every year. His latest novels include the dystopian horror *The Getaway* and the fantasy novel *Epic Ellisons: Cosmos Camp*. He is a founding member of We Need Diverse Books and resides in Virginia with his family.

Photo by Adrienne Giles

Paris Alleyne is a Toronto-based artist. In 2020, he won a prestigious comic book industry Eisner Award as Best Colorist on a Comic Book Series for *Afterlift*, published by Dark Horse. *Static: Up All Night* is his first project for DC Comics.

Photo by Corey Misquita

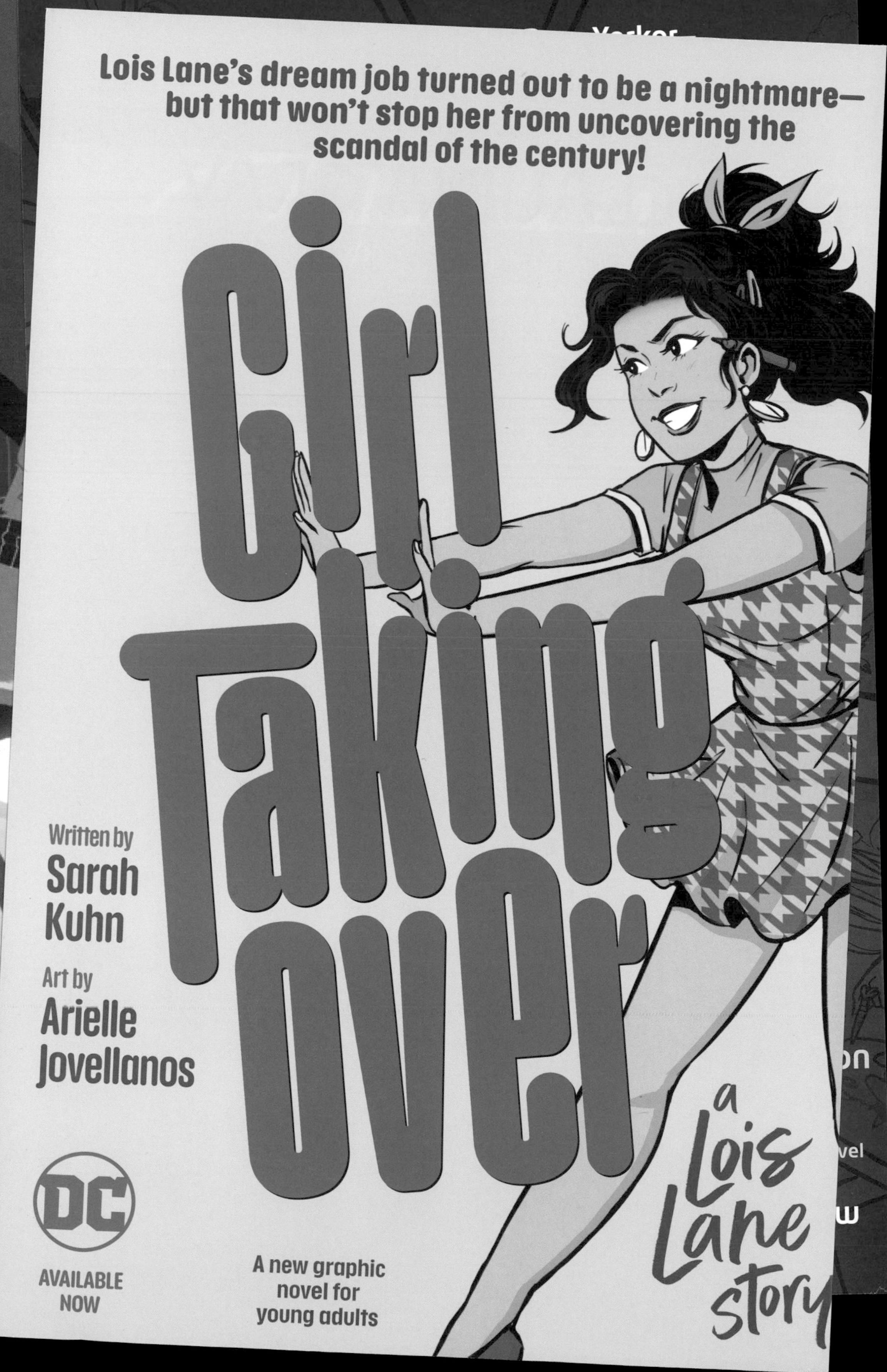
Lois Lane's dream job turned out to be a nightmare—but that won't stop her from uncovering the scandal of the century!
Girl Taking Over
Written by Sarah Kuhn
Art by Arielle Jovellanos
DC
AVAILABLE NOW
A new graphic novel for young adults
a Lois Lane story